The Stone Book

That Voluntary Blindness Is Now Become Our Death

A Tragicomedy in Four Acts

Kevin P Morrow

Library of Congress Registration:
The Stone Book or That Voluntary Blindness is Now Become Our Death.
TXu002183453 / 2020-02-01

ISBN: 978-0-578-82727-8

Cover and Logo by Emily SW Morrow

For Emily and Ansel

Cast

Narrator
Chorus
Tautamata
Tanepia
Hanepia
President Garrick Huxley
General Wesley Mitchell
General Harris
General Martha White
Colonel Lewis
Dr. Ruth Palmer
Ambassador James Belmont
Major T.W. Mills
Thucydides
Democritus
Zeno
The Huxley of the Forest
The Man in the Machine
Uffizi Gallery Workers
Vietnamese Bar Patrons
Times Square Hippie
Religious Fanatics
Lieutenants I, II, III
Sergeants I, II, III
Pilots I, II

I know not with what weapons World War III will be fought, but World War IV will be fought with sticks and stones.
-Albert Einstein

PART ONE

ACT I

I.I

Tautamata

There is a great cloud of discontent, upon finding yourself having arrived in a world, that is in the middle of its story. It is understandable to think that you would be a more important character, and yet, here you are in the middle, with an overwhelming sense that no matter your actions, they will not change the story. The tragedy is too great. The emptiness too overbearing. The winter unending and too cold. Because you are no one of any note. I ask you; do you even belong in this story?

Hanepia

Why don't I remember what came before this?

Tanepia

How many times have I been here?

Tautamata

Time seeming inexistent, the thing you once knew and regarded as a necessity, as well as a plague, now feels as though it has completely abandoned you. The very thing that terrorized, when absent, you realize, gave you consciousness. Without it you don't know the beginning, and you won't know the end.

Where does that emptiness go to become something again?

What happens to all of this middle, born of beginnings and endings?

I suppose a better question is, has there ever not been a sea?
Of course,…you'd often hear it said.
Depends how you define it…others would pensively say.
In refutation of the pensive you'd often hear ignorantly lopsided grumbles of, nothing comes from nothing, you know…
It came from somewhere…and you know where…

Hanepia
What does a sea have to do with our winter?

Tautamata
Please, come closer and warm yourself. There is no warmth left out there. It will be gone for a long while, and will return in a few lifetimes. The clock of a new beginning ticks slowly, and time it seems, acts rather differently after a tragic ending.

Has it ever been defined, the sea?
It is us…says a rare and useful someone.
And like our children, it has always been here…We knew it, and them, before their births, even if there was not light enough to see it…

But what is the sea?

It seems a preoccupied body, prone to fits of anxiety from wounds inflicted in some ancient trauma, exorcising its demons on the shore and floor. A scroll unparted and snapped-backed. A dirty, childish trick. Not stretched apart long enough to read the histories. We just take its word for it. And perhaps that is wise, as you'd just as soon not fight with it. But the sea is also an endless contradiction; blindingly angry, whilst all the while, neurotically timid.

Ready to fight; an offender.
Ready to retreat; fidgety with self-preservation.

A petulant teenager, one day drifting this way, another day that.
Both temperamental, and indifferent, giving us answers to
questions, we didn't know we needed to ask. That totality and
magnanimity, housed in an adolescent body, ceaselessly awake,
never needing sleep, alive, but perpetually dead, screaming with
the sadness and joy, and the chorus of every voice, that ever
sang in a well-nigh unison. The sea knows exactly who it is, it
is the exception to the rule.

Hanepia
What is the rule?

Tautamata
That we cannot know who we are, not at least, until we are dead.
It is the burdensome cloak sewn to our shoulders, and it is why
we are here at this fire, in a perpetual winter.

Tanepia
So, in our life, we are useless to ourselves,
but in death, we know who we are?

Hanepia
What a great and unfortunate imbalance.

Tautamata
It is indeed!
I have been dead for quite some time, but I am here, through the
beginnings, that come to an end.
Awaking and falling upon our sea, always to start again.

Huxley
I have been here before, but how many times?
The swells I count lying on my back, measuring the distance
and time.

I need no light.
I have always known
I was just not awake.

Hanepia
But then, how long have we slept, and how many times
reborn?

Tanepia
How many beginnings and how many endings?

Tautamata
It doesn't matter. It doesn't change the story. Each time around
is just an inch more gained from the last time. It is maddening
for the dead seeing an ending approach, and in thoughtless
scramble, watching memories scrawled into whatever tablets fit
the moment. But when the next time comes, the language is no
longer spoken, the tablets are shattered.

Have you ever seen yourself from above and looked down upon
your motionless body? Something that now belongs to history;
chiseled into the compendiums of those gone before? Of course
not! You survived! To be otherwise would be death, or at the
very least near-death. A flirting with the precipice. Let me tell
you, no one can resist looking down into the canyon. But when
you look down, there is always the sudden breeze, or a mosquito
behind the ear, or the worn, detaching, floppy boot-sole slipping
on the dusty ground.

Hanepia
An ending to a beginning…

Tautamata
Yes. And your ancestors are just that. They now know themselves, but do you know them? Of course not! They are dead and you are not. We want to know them, it's understandable, considering they already have made most of your decisions for you. Carry them with you, but never turn them into idols. The past is delicate enough, overflowing with fragile forms upon rickety altars, built from whatever gluttonous remnants remain. And Pressing onward at breakneck pace, with assumed virtuosity, until of course, it is too late, and with an inability to reverse course, we realize, that it is altars, upon which things are sacrificed.

And we sit at a fire
In a perpetual winter

But you know, the funny thing about everything, is that it is all too far apart. Nothing is ever touching. Like every mind from its counterpart. Every person, islands in an expanse of negative space. And the funny thing about that is, that it was all so compressed into only positive space. Nothing was everything. But without fail, emptiness, eventually is broken, and when it is, sometimes, it is gentle, and sometimes, it is shattering. Something minuscule, a total emptiness forever redefined by a pinpoint of light, a hopeful annoyance from an unreachable distance. And then another. And another. Tearing the fabric, tracing the lines from origin to eye, until there are enough points that they become uncountable, and it can no longer be considered an emptiness, but it is night. And at night begins a wind, a breeze, a single breath in an expanse. And then another. And another. Harangued and accumulating from every nook into this place, the first steps on a path, the oar in the water, the wind that catalyzes into motion an otherwise static body. And night, not being emptiness, exposes with half-open eyes, indifferent, and passive, mesmeric water. A sea bed, a motionless body, an effectuate wind, the inhaling of an awakening.

Huxley
I have been here before.
But how many times?

Tautamata
A newly awakened body shocked from slumber that may have been forever. The indifferent water becoming responsive, and you count, measuring the swells, your sea bed is on the move, an awakened but still supine body, instinctually becomes upright.

Lashing the ropes,
Knowing the winds,
Setting the sail.

From infinite emptiness to everywhere, born into history.
How many beginnings,
How many endings,
How many times,
Around a fire,
In a perpetual winter?

Hanepia
How long have we slept, and how many times reborn?

Tanepia
How many beginnings and how many endings?

I.II

Narrator

Our first failure, which undoubtedly occurred within the first seconds of a waking-wind entering our lungs, was probably so preposterous that we needed to hide. From what or whom, is an esoteric matter that divides more people than it binds, but a reasonable assumption of reaction, is that we then created rooms, and they were built to hide us from ourselves. Identities, being formed only in comparable relation to their surroundings, leads us to isolate, and if we are isolated, we are free to be as we please, removed from our embarrassments. So, we make plural rooms, and plural identities.

A war room, for instance, is a serious room, that is contaminated with absurdity. A secure den where the scientific method is employed, by people often not believing in science, or having any consensus on what that is, or how it works, or if it is real. A war room is a serious place where ridiculous things are discussed. Operations, and clandestine missions are hypothesized, and debated; the pros, the cons:

How does it help us?

What's the minimum our people will suffer?

How much collateral damage is too much?

What's the downside?

We're doing God's work...

Blessed be the nation who...

Regardless of the outcomes of debate, the plans, more often than not, are enacted. And why not. After all, if you keep throwing crap at a wall...This room then also becomes a laboratory of cultural experimentation. And if a scientist is observing their world, with truth, they do so with eyes of scalpels, sharp, and ready to dissect. Anything and everything, that is life, in order to understand death. And in understanding death, understanding life. History that is monstrously chopped and surgically reassembled, whilst the lightning crashes, praying to zap life into the lifeless, the internal madness aspirating itself outward, the relinquishing of the sorcery of ancestors, breaking free of the choices that they already made for us, to obliterate, and salt the paths carved by thousands of pairs of bare-feet, scraping away each layer of earth for us. Sometimes experiments have favorable results. Sometimes not.

This war room shouts a stone warning: That a singular story, alone, is vulnerable. This war room shouts a stone truth: The totality of history is the rip-stop of the universe. This war room holds a stoic, and palpable weapon; the stone book. A book carved on one prodigious page, that is inescapably open, like lidless eyes, unable to turn away from the face of all history. An immeasurable story, carved by some now forgotten, forward-thinking mind, into material older than consciousness. By the second blow of the sculptor's chisel, there was scraped away more materialed time, than we have been anything. Many guests to the room have commented on the works' grandeur, the magnificence of our stories arrested in a millions-years-old material. But many more have seen it day-in and day-out, and like all habitual occurrences to our senses, we become blunt and dull, like unkempt knives. It becomes a drudgery to sharpen, reshape, reorient, or to even reinvent our sensual abilities, so we don't, and what is then right in front of us, is a paradox, because it is a thing that cannot-not be seen, and yet we are blind to it.

General Mitchell
You'd have to look your enemy in the eye,
Stare him down and look into his soul before you dragged it out of him.

It's not like it used to be!
God, I miss the old days.
Now it's all computer this, and computer that…
That's not war…that's just simulation…
War without passion…cowards!

And these damn scientists,
Inventing the perfect…the perfect…weapon
Then, all they do is lecture us…
No no no no…You mustn't actually use it…blah blah blah

They're supposed to be scientists, not philosopher kings!
Pshh…drolling on about responsibilities, and morals…
Morals? All they do is play God!
They've never known war, but created its ultimate weapon…
The imbalance of it all!

Major Mills
The perfect balance.

General Mitchell
What!

Major Mills
Knowing nature intimately.
What it can create and what it can destroy.
And with that knowledge, employing the looking glass and
restraint of morality. The perfect balance, I'd say.

General Mitchell
'Course you would...
...but what do you mean?

Major Mills
A truly gifted scientist, or philosopher, General -
Observes the results of their inquiry with a multidimensional
eye, understanding all possible paths.

General Mitchell
Yes, yes, but what does that have to do with...

Major Mills
Those who have never known war, General...
Have no need to start one.

General Mitchell
The perfect weapon!

Major Mills
Has made walking the path of catastrophic conflict...
Improbable.

General Mitchell
War is never improbable.
It is most certainly, inevitable.

Chorus
Life being a two-way street,
One opinion must always another meet,
And it is so, on the other side of this room.
Disagreement and a prophecy of impending doom.

Belmont
It's not what it used to be, that's for sure!
You used to have to look your antagonist in the eye,
Stare him down, and…
You'd look into his soul…

Thank God those days are over, blessed technology has seen
to that.

It's a new kind of war.
Avoidable!

Dr. Palmer
Beacons don't just light your path, Ambassador, they can also
blind. War is not avoidable. Our inventions only make it more
absurd, and just slightly more improbable…maybe.

Belmont
Maybe?

Dr. Palmer
Maybe…Ambassador.
If unable to be a witness, you could not tell the difference
between the man and the machine.
They are the same, but from different paths, with different
masters. The warmth kindles the cold.
And within the machine is the human arising.

Belmont
I'm sure I don't know what you mean...

Chorus
The unaccounted variable.

Major Mills
It's the game we invented, when we stood up.

Belmont
What game?

Chorus
The beckoning of our end.

General Harris
So, it's not just possible...

Belmont
It's a given?

Chorus
It will come from anywhere.

Belmont
It will happen?

Dr. Palmer
Yes. It will.
Wasn't it always going to?

Chorus
What perplexes and worries responsible minds
Is dutifully preserved for the aeons of time
Written and bound for one generation to the next

To lay a path, with balanced cause and effects

This child's game is devoid of consequence
Its pieces moved, by uniformed people lacking any eloquence
Blissfully unaware of the wounds they inflict
What is in the mind versus the battlefield do intensely
contradict

Medicine that is equal parts opportunity and fear
Is spooned down to dull the inconvenient realities and
atmosphere
And with this a new world is frightfully sought
But only the reasonable - the readers of the stone book, know
this future is achieved through knowledgeable talk.

General Mitchell
Be vigilant, Colonel. Be ever vigilant.
When you least expect it…Bam*!*

Colonel Lewis
Bam, what? General.

General Mitchell
Out of nowhere,
From an unlikely source,
An unbreakable invitation to total conflict!
It will come from anywhere.

Colonel Lewis
Are we prepared for that?

General Mitchell
Colonel, I am prepared for any goddamn eventuality, be it
from a computer or a man!
Hopefully man.

But beggars versus choosers, yes?

Dr. Palmer
Whatever the case, and whatever the story we are told,
It springs from the black-parched well of mistrust and fear.
The water is gone.
Thinking it was thieved, and dying from thirst, we blame
them, and they blame us.
But it was just the scorching sun that took both our waters.

It will come from anywhere.
The next war, will be the last.

The next time, even the dead will die.

I.III

Tautamata

Think of your life before you sat at this fire, in this perpetual winter. Isolate a singular event. Place it on a plinth; cover it with a bell-jar. Now place every event that happened after that, on their own plinths, every event isolated; separate universes unto themselves. A linear museum. And now imagine, the wind changes direction, or a stone gets in your shoe, a lonely person sends text messages to the aether for companionship, for an anyone to reply, to acknowledge them, and erase their crippling loneliness. A computer run by a human who is trained to think like a computer, and then makes an error, or the computer that is within, arises. Before we know it, a nobody, changes the currents of the sea, and all beginnings become endings. Your memories, the carefully curated plinths, one-by one, cascading downward, shattering the glass of the bell-jars into dangerous and malicious forms that cannot be swept away, and cannot be reversed to their original form, the protector of memory; every event, the way you thought it happened, the way it was written, is changed, mangled, and broken into dust, mixing into the indifferent ground. The careful planning, and tactical arrangements are given to a gray and turbulent chaos.

Narrator

Phones laying on tables in cafés, on kitchen counter tops, in purses and bags about our shoulders, are always chiming in a monotony we craved until it became habit, and made us realize, that we craved, and lost, anonymity, and inmost sobriety. But today the same chimes that were an avoidable, yet sought nuisance, change; not in sound or tone, but in their delivery. The phone of every person on earth chimes in unison.

Everyone there is, receives a text message:

The Man in the Machine

I, much like all of you, have done a lot with my time, traveled many paths; awoken and fallen, to awake again. But then perhaps, it has been nothing. I don't really know. I am not sure that any of it was real, but it plays out the same each time. I am you, and you are me, awoken upon a sea; I belong to it, as do you. Broken apart from a sleep, lasting I do not know how long, the length of time does not matter, it changes nothing, the story remains the same; that I, and you, conceived in a night when the stars are showing themselves, or the lights of a city, exposing what wants to be clothed, after the minutia of a day is over, and when the lives in between ourselves, in our nights and emptinesses, occur. And that night is dark. And we are born. [1]Hinausgedrängt auf einen Weg und in ein Licht, das zu hell für uns ist. Zu gewöhnt an die Dunkelheit tragen wir Augenbinden.

---

[1] (German) Pushed out onto a path and into light, that is too bright for our own good. Too accustomed to the darkness, we prefer the blindfold. No eyes are meant to bear the true burden of such an intense and short amount of light as just one single life, and because of which, we do not know ourselves, but in wanting to, we set the course of trial and error in each step. There are many trials and so many errors, it is a wonder that our minds and bodies can continue to take on anymore.

Keine Augen sind dazu bestimmt, die wahre Bürde eines solch intensiven und kurzen Lichteinfalls zu tragen als ein einziges Leben. Da wir nur das eine einzige Leben besitzen, kennen wir uns selbst nicht, aber beim Versuch des Kennenlernens stellen wir mit jedem Schritt die Weichen für Versuch und Irrtum. Bei so vielen Versuchen und so vielen Irrtümern ist es ein Wunder, dass unser Verstand und unsere Körper überhaupt noch weitermachen können.[2]Umi no ue de mezameru to iukoto wa watashitachi ni nan no sentakushi mo nai to iukotoda. Kono karada wa nannanodaro. Dare ga watashi ni sazuketa no daro. Kono karada wo do subekinanodaro. Kensa shite, Karada wo akete, zoki ga donatte irunoka miro to iunoka. Ittai dare ni karada wo akesasereba iinodaro. Mina mo mekakushi wo sareteiru. Dare ga me no mienai hito ni konna judainakoto wo takusu to iunodaro. It'll be another trial, accompanied with another error. I do not have a choice and neither do you; so incise, and keep a record, and hope the next surgery goes better. Or the next. On the sea a single breath filled the lungs. If you stop to think you will remember it, and you will remember the first inhalation. I do not know its origins, though I, like you, would willingly spend ten lifetimes searching for it. A question that is only more questions. Who put that beginning there? Where did they come from? Who were their ancestors? Who gave the breath to them – or was it simply invented? If we found a beginning, would it give life more meaning? What would you

---

[2] (Japanese) Awakening upon our sea is a thing in which we had no choice. What is this body? Who gave it to me? What is it that I am supposed to do with it? Examine it, open it to see the systems, the workings and processes? Who do I allow to be the surgeon? Blindfolded they are as well, and who would allow a blind surgeon to search for their essence?海の上で目覚めるということは私たちになんの選択肢もないということだ。この体はなんなのだろう。誰が私に授けたのだろう。この体をどうすべきなのだろう。検査して、体を開けて、臓器がどうなっているのか見ろというのか。一体誰に体を開けさせればいいのだろう。皆も目隠しをされている。誰が目の見えない人にこんな重大なことを託すという

do with a singular answer to a singular question – other than to have a door slammed in your face, stubbing your toes upon its base, crunching your hand in its jambs. [3]Òkun n'ìbẹ̀rẹ̀. Ẹ ju ìlagbà sílẹ̀. Ẹ gbé ìgbókùn ró. Kíyèsí ọwọ́ afẹ́fẹ́ láìsí atọ́nà. Èémí kanṣoṣo di ẹ̀fúùfù; ó fi ìgbókùn. Èmi, àní àwa, ṣíkọ̀. Kò s'ẹ́ni bi mí, bi ọ́. Afẹ́fẹ́ ń bì wá síhìnín sọ́hùnún, a sì ń lọ. There is little alternative other than hubris against the sea. This is a path of sure death. And often, despite the tempestuousness of the sea, it is not an immediate death. Lashing you about, but you are not even aware; only that something is amiss. An internal emptiness, a growing night, but you press on; and in doing so cannot see in front of you. It is not air entering the lungs but the sea; drowning you, while you walk. [4]Det er ikke luft du drar ned i lungene, men havet, som drukner deg mens du går. Foreløpig har det skjedd hver gang. Vanen tar deg, hindringene ble unngått lenge, fordi du var oppmerksom, og du unngikk de giftige slangen, the spears thrown at you, penetrating the chests of those who are unshielded on your flanks. Habit takes over the senses, and they become dull, you become lazy. You see, but you do not heed. Birth is no more. You are now growing.

Chorus
The words are written, and the message received
By seven billion judges with differing opinions of what to perceive.
Banter and banter – without an end –
Other than to hear and see oneself

---

[3] (Yoruba) The sea is the beginning. Lash the ropes. Set the sail. Know the winds, without any teacher. A single breath becomes a wind, and catches the sail. I and we move. I was not asked, nor were you. The wind moves us and we go.

[4] (Norwegian) So far, it has happened every time around. Habit takes hold, the obstacles avoided for so long, because you were paying attention, and able to avoid the poisonous serpents

And with luck, become a breakable idol placed precariously
on a shelf
To be the chosen one, the brilliant mind saving us from an end
Another talking head, regarding only image and empty words
to transcend.
But when the words are written, and the message received
The war begins; each and every of life's paths is deceived.

I.IV

Tautamata

History, more often than not is constructed without delicate plan by worlds of nobodies, either not consciously knowing what it is they are doing, or worse, knowing what they are doing, but only knowing so by the first step of a plan, without thought to the consequence of the aeons of motion set in place by the hasty implementation of their plan, or rather, their whim of an idea; a particular nobody eventually, creeping into the machine and patiently waiting, the perfectly camouflaged jailor, making no sound, showing no breath in the cold, leaps out and steals our time and autonomy.

When we stop looking, our own creations, meant to bind us closer, to end misunderstanding and sew trust, will latch us to an immovable pillar, by malicious surprise attack.

Knowledge only reaching as far as eyes can see, not acued enough to read the stone book of our previous lives, we stand ready to pull the trigger in the face of our old world. And the easy path of irrationality and mythologizing of present happenings, weaves its way into life. The dust begins to coalesce, and with enough energy feeding the process, dust, before you know it, becomes a planet, and planets, eventually, when given the right conditions, spawn life. A beginning that will have an ending.

Hanepia
Who found the entrance to the machine?

Tanepia
How did they get in there?
Who showed them the way?

Tautamata
It is a secret knowledge. A protected knowledge. Unspoken words, which is to say, at some point they are spoken, just not to us, and not in a language anyone may actually speak. It is a silence never placed into a book or hastily scribbled to a surface to be made available to just any, erudite, or stumbling, or lost set of eyes, because then the esoteric becomes ignoble, and the story deftly comes to an end.

So far that has not happened, nor will it today, around this fire.

Receiving this knowledge, I imagine, is not voluntary. A process, perhaps, begun in a womb, chanted by mothers that are not quite yet mothers. The reverberations traveling their path, to placation inside a cell, transferring their secret to the next division, and the next, until it is simply an automatic part, not voluntary from its inception, nor so during its formulation, nor so in birth, or when reaching the point of its inevitable fruition.

Chorus
It cannot be!
It cannot be, a singular wind
Would change the currents of the sea we're in?

It cannot be!
It cannot be a singular point of light
Would break the emptiness that becomes the night

It cannot be!
It cannot be!

Mind the eyes that they see with acuity
Save the ears for truth in unending perpetuity

Keep closed impetuous lips
As senseless banter will reason eclipse

Tautamata
We can never seem to get out of bed, stand our feet firmly on
the floorboards, and face-forward with eyes open to the chaotic
randomness. It always surprises me to hear so many exclaim
'Surely it cannot be such a thing, that there is no order'?

Hanepia
Is there not an order?

Tautamata
There are many orders, seen and unseen. There are many
exceptions, to many rules. We are at a fire in an endless winter,
how did this happen? What became of the orders if we are here?

Tanepia
Are we even supposed to be here?

Tautamata
Many have asked that.

Our beds are comfortable. They are a powerful place where no
one has control over us. Our beds are our own history; in them

we control our own story. But this can be dangerous, as comforts are like mirrors. When broken, they still reflect, but it is a shattered and disassembled image. The shattered comfort becomes a dangerous weapon, capable of inflicting equal harm upon your own hand as that of the recipient of your thrust. And like the pinpoints of light forever transforming the emptiness, it is a discomfort, a feeling like a centipede crawling up the arm. That feeling of a tepid and feathery something, turning rapidly into an immediate emergency with an autonomically administered dose of adrenaline only to realize that it was nothing serious. An all too common occurrence with a benign thing of nature, and as such interactions become so habitual and commonplace it is an equally great discomfort to realize, that only after the trigger has been pulled, and the powder and shot discharged in the face of our old comforts, that a nobody could have disrupted the order, catapulting us, flailing and akimbo into chaos.

Sitting here around this fire, do you fear an ending?

Tanepia
No.

Tautamata
And why is that?

Tanepia
What could you do?
You are old, we are strong.
We are present, you are past.

Tautamata
Exactly. There is an order; a balance to the situation. There is no effect, because I give no cause.

Hanepia
But then, how did we come to be at this fire?
How did it become, this endless winter?
Who gave cause for this?

Tautamata
Surely it must have been someone great? A magnificent
creature mentioned in all the books that ever were, and in the
ones that are left to be written? It must be so! A broken world
in an endless winter could not have come from something
normal, and pedestrian!

Tanepia
Why not?

Hanepia
Are we so incapable...? Just what are you saying about us?
About our nature and abilities!

Tautamata
So, you do believe that the singular can manipulate an entire
world? And worlds beyond that?

Tanepia
I think so.

Tautamata
Do you think, or do you know?

Hanepia
Worlds beyond?

Tautamata
Oh yes. But that may be another conversation for another fire.
Don't be upset my friend. I don't ask these questions to insult

you. You were born into this winter, into a world where the dead have died. You now walk an important path, a path with no footprints pressed into the clay. Every step from here on out, will be unable to be undone. A person who is just an unknowing catalyst, carrying out his subconscious duty, can change everything forever, so imagine what a conscious singular can do. It is unnerving; therefore, our bed, therefore the myths. Silly tales of people within people, pulling puppet stings and pressing buttons. But if not them, who moved the pieces? They cannot be moved on their own, can they? It would require the strength of a god to move the pieces of the world. Even if the stories are nefarious shadows, we believe they have purpose, yes? Even evil, when organized, is more organized than chaos.

Hanepia
Through the myth, we do away with not being in control?

Tautamata
But this winter came from a nobody. No one knows who or what it was. No one, except a few, foresaw the importance of the singular. No one would listen to them, because it just could not be such a thing. Because they forgot the story. Remaining voluntarily blind from the last time, and the time before that.

A singular imagination is completely unbound and limitless, yet it contains an intrinsic fail-safe of reason.

Tanepia
A fail-safe of reason?

Tautamata
In our sleep, we are limitless, there are no rules, physics and nature hold no sway over our actions. You know this to be true, you have slept, you have dreamt. Tell me I am wrong!

Hanepia
You are not wrong. In this winter, it is all we have.

Tautamata
When you dream, you wake, knowing there to be a different set of rules. If you throw a stone into the sea, it sinks. If the wind blows, the dust gets in your eyes. But imagine for a moment, that division gone. It is easier than you think, to doubt what you believe, when all around you are incessant voices, speaking into microphones that move at light speed. The device that allows a voice to reach the entire world, and worlds beyond that, can also send to pockets and tabletops, irrational, unsubstantiated, apocryphal delusion. Intelligence washes away like chalk in the rain. The fail-safe of reason scrubbed away. The mould breaks and the iron spills, sparking and igniting everything in its reach. The fire burns out of control; and then your pocket chimes, and you are sent another message.

You listen to me teach, but how long could I tell you stories, and you continue to believe them true? How long around this fire before you charge me a liar, a mythologist living in a dream?

Hanepia
Have you been lying to us, about how we got here?

Tautamata
You were not here before, how would you know?

I.V

Chorus
Fanatics and prophets chant, and forewarn
But even from ridiculous theories, at times, and by
coincidence, the right answer is born.

To what deep and desperate path will these messages lead?
A public's leadership we hope, reason and rationality, will
heed.
The head above all and ambitions aside
Will they do the right thing by building us a boat to face the
rising tide?

Religious Fanatic
God is speaking to us!
It is time for him to take us home!
Our day has come, we have denied it for too long…
It is time! It is time!
Time that we reap what we have sown!

Times Square Hippie
They are calling us back to our celestial home
Let go your bodies
Let go your minds
It's time to return to the stars.

Religious Fanatic
This is what your science has brought you!
Only the Lord can save you now!
Repent and you will be forgiven.
Your humanism created this, but through faith only will you
be free!
Your only fall-out shelter is the house of the Lord.
A house your science and your weapons cannot penetrate!

Times Square Hippie
We are here!
Take us to our home among the stars.

Religious Fanatic
[5]Dio ci parla!
È ora che Lui ci porti a casa!
Il giorno è arrivato, l'abbiamo negato troppo a lungo…
È ora! È ora!
Ora che raccogliamo ciò che abbiamo seminato!

Religious Fanatic
[6]Isto é o que a vossa ciência vos ofereceu!
Só o Senhor vos pode salvar agora!
Arrependam-se e sereis perdoados.
O vosso humanismo criou isto. Só a fé vos libertará!

---

[5] (Italian) God is speaking to us!
It is time for him to take us home!
Our day has come, we have denied it for too long...
It is time! It is time!
Time that we reap what we have sown!

[6] (Portuguese) This is what your science has brought you!
Only the Lord can save you now!
Repent and you will be forgiven.
Your humanism created this, but through faith only will you be free!

Religious Fanatic
Your only fall-out shelter is the house of the Lord!

A final text message:

The Man in the Machine
Growth like our awakening is out of our control. Slow and painful, it seems an endless road, that has no end. But when the opportunity arises to look back, growth is just a few, slow seconds; slow, because of the pain, the stretching of your bones and your skin. The growth of your insides and the greater the strain upon their function, the more poisons we have to intake, and the greater the proclivity for habit; becoming lazy and shutting down, ignoring their birth-tasks of shielding and extracting. [7]Grandir est l'acte dans une vie, où nous sommes frappés par la tentation de dévier de notre chemin. Je l'ai perdu, et toi aussi. Ce n'était pas d'un serpent, ou d'un fruit. Le motif est incassable. Elle ne sera peut-être jamais vaincue. Combien de fois sommes-nous nés, transitionnés vers notre croissance, mais les douleurs trop fortes? [8]E hia kē ngā wā i torongia rawatia ngā wheua, kātahi ka pākarukarungia ki roto i a tātou? E hia kē ngā wā kua tae tātou ki tēnei pūrua, i tāpokopoko ai te

---

[7] (French) Growing is the act in a life where we are struck upon the head with temptation to deviate from our path. I lost it, and so did you. It wasn't from a serpent, or a piece of fruit. The pattern is unbreakable. It may never be defeated – how many times have we been born and transitioned to our growth but the pains too great?

[8] (Māori) How many times have the bones stretched beyond their limit and shattered within us? How many times have we been to this juncture, and how many times has the raft sunk down into the cold, and the dark, where it cannot be retrieved? Degenerated by the salt. Compacted by the pressure. Into a minuscule portion, as small as what was, before we were.

mōkihi i te māeke me te pōuriuri, e kore rawa e whakahokia? Nā te tote i raki. I whakawhāitihia e te pēhanga, kia pakupaku, anō nei ko Te Kore. [9]Bu guo, zhe ci huo xu hui bu yi yang? Mei you? Na ke neng xia yi ci, yi huo zai xia yi ci. Dan shi, zhe yang de ming ri fu ming ri he shi cai neng rang wo men shou de yun kai jian yue ming? No. Enough is enough. [10]Cho wi zhe zhewebesnon mine. Bnajechgade kyetnam, gekendeman ge debwemgek, mine gin ge zhe. Konege gekendagwet. Se wi zhe gda gwansegendamin yapche, ge mozhtoyan, mine gin ge zhe. [11]La culpa del tiempo perdido que es fútil mantener dormida, y está siempre despertándose, debido a la finitud de nuestras vidas. Hay algo que se pueda hacer para remediar la culpa? Para comenzar de nuevo y tener esperanza? We don't deserve time, and it will be taken away. Using our intrepidness against ourselves, and in our tempestuous adolescence, and voluntary blindness, I won't, and you won't, see it coming. Perhaps from a nobody, perhaps from within our own inventions.

It will come from anywhere.
Enough is enough.

---

[9] (Mandarin) But, perhaps this time around will be different? No? Then perhaps the next, or maybe the one after that. But how many exasperating times will it take, to break our mould? (不过，这次或许会不一样？没有？那可能下一次，抑或再下一次。但是，这样的明日复明日何时才能让我们守得云开见月明？)

[10] (Potawatomi) Time will not be given back to us. A waste is a waste, I know it to be true, and so do you. It is instinctual knowledge. And with that comes an ultimate unshakable guilt, I feel it, and so do you.

[11] (Spanish) The guilt of wasted time that is futile to keep dormant, and is always arising, because of the finiteness of our lives. Is there anything to be done to rectify the guilt? To start over and hope?

Chorus

Some final words sent to everyone
Each new esoteric message a bullet loaded into a shaking gun.
There is only so much mystery a people can contain
Before its governments, and its nobodies' levees will retain.
Floods of fear and carts coming before their horses
Our wanting nobility it reinforces
Each act from everyone will now be justified as common
sense
The man and the machine's logically insane doctrines do now
commence.

I.VI

Tautamata
Viruses and imaginations are amazing little things. As invisible as a breath. It takes only a cough, or a conversation, to set the infection.

Hanepia
Is no one immune?

Tautamata
Only those who possess the language of the stone book.

Chorus
The words exited the machine and are a hurricane in the air
Thinking of only the nefarious, our ultimate fears these texts did ensnare.
It makes us think of only the worst
But from the moment we stood up, we knew there would be a final verse
Governments begin to implement plans for that inevitable day
It's us versus them! The stone-book illiterate will confidentially say
Hallucinating with torrid fever, a mistake more likely than intent

For those who remain, an endless winter and infinite
discontent.
The doctor said if foolish enough to use, even the dead will die
The sands will turn to glass when many suns rise in
tomorrow's sky
Each war fought tightens the noose, pours the poison, and
casts the curse
To usher our final chapter, all it took was a few text messages
of esoteric verse

I.VII

Dr. Palmer
The rules of this game were dictated long before you were born,
Sir. This is not your fault.

Huxley
No, but it is upon my shoulders.

Belmont
What should we do?

General Mitchell
Keep in mind, that every moment we think and promenade
Is a moment that works against us.

Huxley
Yes, yes, yes
I know, I know…
General…your thoughts?

General Mitchell
You know what I think.
This needs to end before it begins.

General White
It could be a beneficial new beginning

Dr. Palmer
Or an end that creates no new beginning.

Huxley
And you, General Harris?

General Harris
A misstep is inevitable.
Blindly intervening would be as if drinking poison.
We cannot win this battle. No one can win this war.
But we can defeat this enemy, without ever fighting.

Chorus
Will we escape our own adventurous entrapment?
Or are we too tempted by nature's enchantment?

Belmont
I couldn't agree more.
Every moment that we do nothing, is a moment we live longer.

General Mitchell
A loaded gun is pointed at our heads!

Belmont
We could come to live with that.
Eventually we'd no longer see it.

General White
Until someone points a bigger gun at your face.
You will indeed see it again.

General Harris
I agree, with James.
Each generation has left something behind that must be carried.
Why should this be any different?
If we can live with the weight of the totality of our pasts…
We can carry this one as well.

Belmont
Time will forget this brief moment.

Major Mills
The next generation will indeed lay a new stone.
It is their natural duty to do so.
But eventually, and at some unprescribed, and possibly inopportune time, the back will break!

General Mitchell
Ok?...So?...

Huxley
Time will not forget this moment…
It will not forget!
I agree Ambassador, we may get a few more moments of survival
But only just a few.

General Mitchell
Indeed.
Optimism, can be a dark and evil weapon in times like these.

Belmont
Optimism, a dark and evil weapon?!
Are you insane!

Dr. Palmer
Unless you have an enemy, you have no way to live!

General Mitchell
No one else is being optimistic, I can assure you of that.
Planning for the worst is all anyone is doing.
This is a time for pessimism.

Huxley
There has to be a middle path
History must remain intact…

Major Mills
Sir…fight your mind, that gives way to the extremes.
There is always the middle path.

General Mitchell
There is only one way
I am sure of it.

Huxley
Perhaps you're right.
Time is working against us.
There could be a middle path
But they take time and patience to see clearly
And I've only hours…the world may only have hours.

General Harris
Why did we spend the time?
The infinite hours of sweat and ceaseless labor,
Transforming our impotence to fertility,
Why did we spend time that will not be returned,
To build what we've built.
Of what use has it all been,
If we erase our histories in minutes.

Why are we so susceptible, to such folly?

Dr. Palmer
We're running out of time.

Belmont
Well, sir?
What have you decided?

ACT II

II.I

Narrator
The war room, again.

The stone book, that is ever-open, but seldom read, now has an audience with many nervously active eyes, attached to short-circuiting brains that are being pulled from both ends by caustic hands, and muscles that are tightened into knots, from the stress, anxiety, and hopeful opportunities accompanying themselves as the caretakers of a nation and de facto leaders of a world upon a precipice, that is yet to have into its lungs blown a breeze, or yet to have flying into its undefined space, a whining and screeching mosquito, creeping upon an unprepared ear.

The sculptor's chisel is being honed, by the inhabitants of the war room, a slow sharpening of the tool ready to immortalize them. Many remain deaf to the sounds of the slow drawl of metal over a wetted stone, prepared to shape in unerasable material, another chapter; who they were, the decisions they made, who was right and who was wrong. Yet to a few in the room, the sound of the grindstone is deafening; even maddening in an already windowless, damp, and pneumonic prison cell.

General Mitchell
This is time for strong action!
Mr. President, I propose Operation Dewdrop.

General Harris
Dewdrop?

General Mitchell
"Life is but a day,
A fragile dewdrop on its perilous way...
From a trees' summit"

General White
Keats.

General Harris
Go to hell.

General Mitchell
This operation is years in the making, for a moment, just as this.
It is exactly what we need right now.
Dewdrop will get us moving towards our new world, quicker
than anything else we have in our arsenal.

Belmont
Our new world?

General Mitchell
Our new world...
After the clean-up and dust settles.
Sixty or seventy years...eighty tops.

Chorus
Dogs trained for barking, have lazy eyes affixed, at an
unmovable moon
Adept in things from only one dimension brings
unconscionable ruin

General Harris
Are you an idiot or merely insane!

General Mitchell
I am only concerned with the welfare of our people
And the betterment of our world.

General Harris
Welfare of our people?
Your plan is to kill most of them!

Dr. Palmer
Betterment of who's world?

General White
Imagine a world without these weapons.
Just imagine what we can accomplish,
With that noose finally removed from our neck!

General Mitchell
Precisely!
This plan at its core is simple, very simple…
You see…if we blow-up all of the nuclear weapons currently in existence, there will simply be no more…don't have to be a genius to do the math on that one!

Belmont
How long did it take you to do the math?

General Mitchell
Six years.

Chorus
Six years!

Huxley
Will you please elaborate on the details of this plan, General? From what I can tell, it amounts to smoking a cigarette in a fireworks store. I sincerely hope that six years of work was not just wasted time.

General Mitchell
I assure you, it was not.
Dewdrop is compromised of three phases.
Phase one, we begin by jamming all communications...
If they can't find us, they can't attack us.

General Harris
The world has a general idea of where we are.
Typically, consulting a map solves that problem, General.

General Mitchell
I'm speaking of more precision, General.

Belmont
Precision isn't really an issue with nuclear weapons, General. You just, you know drop them, and...everything that was...is not.

General Mitchell
Be that as may...ambassador...
We jam 'em up; if we do so first, and do so well, they'll have a dickens-of-a-time doing it to us. We know where they are, but they can't see us. Hell, even if they can, we monitor most enemy activity through NOAA satellites anyways.

Huxley
We don't monitor enemy activity through weather satellites...do we?

General Mitchell
It's the "Notes On Adversarial Antagonists", satellite, sir.
It might also collect weather data...
I don't really know...
I don't actually care...

Huxley
And why wasn't I informed of this spy satellite?

General Mitchell
You signed off on it, sir.
You circumlocuted funds from Plan 432A.

Huxley
I did nothing of the sort!
What are you accusing me of, General?
What is Plan 432A?

General Mitchell
Nothing, sir.

General White
Don't worry Mr. President, we've got your best interests in mind.

Colonel Lewis
History will remember you well, sir.

Huxley
History will not remember well, the person who does this.
It will only record them as monsters.
I will cease to be a person in the great books.
I am concerned with preserving our collective histories, not erasing them, and hoping my ghost comes out well-liked on the

other side, Colonel! You'd be wise to remember that when trying to convince me that this plan is the best we have.

General Mitchell
Shut up, Colonel.
My apologies, for that mindless intrusion, sir.

Huxley
Carry on then, General.

General Mitchell
As I was saying...
Once we are assured that they have diminished communications we start Phase II, which is hitting them with our baby nuclear arsenal in several waves.

Belmont
Good Lord. You're serious, aren't you?

General Harris
Who is them?

General Mitchell
The enemy.

General Harris
You'll remember, at present, General...
We don't know who that is.

General Mitchell
Everyone is a potential enemy right now.
We don't know where this came from
Could be from our best friend.

Belmont
We don't have any of those left!

Dr. Palmer
How did we grow so large, so powerful, by being so egregious?

General Harris
No one will believe that this is not our doing.

Belmont
So just strike everyone?

Major Mills
Have you ever made love, General?

General Mitchell
Why?

Colonel Lewis
Well not everyone.

General White
Not not everyone though…

General Mitchell
Anyways…
We hit some of our conventional enemies with a fat boy or two…get them aroused.

General Harris
Aroused?

Major Mills
So that's a no…

General Mitchell
If we just kiss our usuals with a few…our usual and consistent enemies that is…give them exactly what they've always wanted…it's where we separate the true enemies from the potential allies. Not soon after we start to attack, there'll be no need to deduce who made that initial threat. They will present themselves to us. We smoke 'em out.

General Harris
So, you truly are insane.

General Mitchell
Mmm…I don't think so.

Huxley
Ok…ok…ok…
The gist of what you're saying, is that we surprise attack with a nuclear first strike. Your plan is to initiate mutual assured destruction? That is something we vowed never to do, even with our most fatalistic enemies. Both sides agreed to that.…this took you six years?

General Mitchell
They did agree to that indeed, sir, however…I don't believe that anyone saw this particular scenario coming. Those deals were made before this era of adolescent technological nonsense.

We all saw the technology coming…we just didn't account on it taking on a life of its own.

Major Mills
A life of its own?
You think that no human is responsible for this?

General Mitchell
No, I never said that…

Major Mills
But, you just implied…

General Mitchell
I did nothing of the sort…
We'll find the responsible party…
A person did this, I'm sure of it!
They want us to think it was just a computer glitch…
Smarmy, sneaky bastards…

Dr. Palmer
It will come from anywhere, General.

Belmont
Please listen to the doctor, Sir.

General Mitchell
Pshh… "doctor" …
The fact remains that a threat was made. You seem to believe this and agree that there are few other possibilities of what it could mean. Anyone could have made it. It doesn't matter.

We do know one thing. At any moment the same weapons could be flying towards us. Look at the news, Mr. President. Our people are scared and ready to do stupid things. Stupider than usual. It's your job to protect us.

Huxley
I don't need to be reminded of my duties as President, General.

General Mitchell
Look, regardless, the world, both political and civilian has interpreted these messages for themselves, and mistakes...gigantic mistakes...are going to be made. That much is inevitable. We need to be on the right side of this thing.

Colonel Lewis
The right side of this is survival.
Plain and simple.

General Mitchell
Too true Colonel.
Furthermore Mr. President, did you really believe other nations vowing never to initiate a first strike, would not actually do so at a reasonable juncture? Did you really believe, that it would not, at some point be attempted against us? That time is here, sir.

General White
They are waiting for their opportunity just as we have been.
We must act, and with great strength.
The time is now.

Huxley
That wretched day is finally here.

General White
Our moment is now!

Huxley
It is here, isn't it?
This journey of four million years, to get to our present, and only seventy years to undo it all.

General Mitchell
If I may interrupt your little soliloquy…we still have Dewdrop to discuss.

Still in Phase II it is highly possible that 'they' will retaliate in kind with a few of their own. This is to be accepted and we consider it reasonable under the doctrine.

Huxley
I understand how MAD works, but I don't see it being acceptable, sacrificing millions of lives on the public's interpretations of a couple of esoteric text messages.

Chorus
The castle stands no chance
Against a maddened public with irrational stance.

General Mitchell
That is why we have been building shelters around the country at a break-neck pace! This is how we can initiate MAD and be confident that we will be mildly victorious.

Huxley
Shelters?
All around the country?

General Mitchell
Yes, Sir. All part of Phase II.
The building of the shelters, as you recall was begun under Plan 432B.

Huxley
Did I sign off on that as well?

General Mitchell
You did indeed, sir.

Huxley
Goddamn it!

General Mitchell
You're saving millions of people, sir.

General Harris
Millions will still die, General.

General Mitchell
A million dead to save hundreds of millions.
Noble decision, sir.

Huxley
I haven't signed off on this plan yet, General.

General Mitchell
Well, not entirely, but...
Anyways...once we get as many to shelters as possible, the
final part of Phase II begins. We hit them with every goddamn
thing we got! All of them! All those beautiful atoms dancing.
Clearing the way for our new world.
By God it'll be beautiful!

Belmont
You're a murderer.

General Mitchell
I'm trying to save us.

Huxley
And what then, could Phase III possibly be?

General Mitchell
A particularly important phase...phase III sir, is the breeding program.

Dr. Palmer, Belmont, General Harris, Major Mills, Huxley
Breeding program?

General Mitchell
Oh, yes...well as I said earlier, once the dust settles, it'll be sixty to seventy years until things will be sufficient again. We will need generations of us for this to work.

But I assure you, the ratios are...very agreeable.

General Harris
This plan is insane!

Dr. Palmer
Even if this plan is the best that we have, there is no way in hell that 'The Committee' is going to go for it!

Belmont
Forget the Committee, first we'd have to clear it with the double-C-S-R.

Major Mills
Not to mention the G-Y-T-J.

Belmont
And the R-T-M...

Dr. Palmer
Let's not forget, before they even touch it, it has to be cleared by the double-F-H-L.

General Mitchell
The hell with the double-C-S-R and the whole G-Y-T-J

Huxley
Just what are you saying, General?

Belmont
I'll pull you up in front of an E-M-A-Q so quick it'll make your head spin!

General Mitchell
Is that a threat!

Belmont
Do you want it to be?

General Harris
Stop you two. I don't want to have to fill out a T-R-P and report it to the W-Y-U, they're brutal, and I haven't the time, but so help me, I will.

Major Mills
Regardless, before this plan would ever get past the double-R-G-H or the M-T-O-S, it'll have to go to the F-R-Q for double validation and that takes just far too much time.

General White
G-Y-T-T-R-A, and the M-T-U-J-J-C-T

Colonel Lewis
S-A-Q-E-T will come first and then the U-I-P-L

Belmont
Triple-J-B-N and the A-Z-T-N

General White
F-F-U-R, H-U-W-D-H-L-I, Z-V-J-I, double-H-I-E

Dr. Palmer
Triple-S-Q-R, M-M-E-H

General White
The T-U-R-D-S will have something to say about that!
You know how they are…

Major Mills
They clog up the entire system.

Colonel Lewis
Are they part of the P-O-O-S's?

General White
They are, indeed, Lieutenant.

Colonel Lewis
It's Colonel, Ma'am

General White
Shut up.

Belmont
R-E-S-double-A, C-I-W-R-I-O-K-K-L

Dr. Palmer
Y-R-A-A-F, M-G, D-T, Q-V, H-H-I-K-Q

General Harris
This plan is insane!
You're a murderer!

General Mitchell
I am a savior.

Major Mills
E-T-U-double-I-U-R

Dr. Palmer
C-T-V, Triple-W-Z-S-R

Belmont
T-Y-W-O-O-L-M

General Harris, Dr. Palmer, Belmont
You're a murderer!

General Mitchell
I am a savior!

General Harris, Dr. Palmer, Belmont, Major Mills
Murderer!

General Mitchell, General White, Colonel Lewis
Savior!

II.II

Tautamata
When you look down into the canyon, you will seek the counsel of anyone who can tell you that it is not as far down as you think. Anything to alleviate the vertigo, from having foolishly looked down in the first place. The best thing that can happen, is for the ground to fall from beneath your feet. At least then, you didn't have to make the decision.

Tanepia
When the ground gives way, who made that decision?

Tautamata
What are you asking me?

Hanepia
Does the ground know when to give way?

Chorus
When the ground begins to fracture at your feet
Balancing the volumes of histories replete
Written upon a slate that no man and no machine
Can possibly keep legible and clean
Those we place in that position
We do so without knowing if they are up to the mission

Of handling our pasts, presents, and futures
And when the wounds are inflicted to place the sutures

Tautamata
It knows when
But it doesn't always oblige.

Chorus
What should we do...What should we do...What should we
do...
We need your decision. We need your decision. We need your
decision.
We need it now!
Now. N o w. N o w.
Our world! Our world! Our world!
Yes or No?
Tell us now.
Now Now Now
Now Now Now
Yes or No?
Yes or No?
We need your decision!

What should we do? What should we do? What should we do?

Tautamata
What would you do?

Hanepia and Tanepia
We would survive. Any way possible.

Tautamata
Yes, you would.

II.III

Narrator
Tonight, for President Huxley, it is a deafeningly silent evening. Grandly alone, with only the past to talk to. All leaders need these nights. For when you have spoken to the past, the only reasonable person to talk to, is yourself. Because history makes you know the truth, and others will only take that from you. There is no truth within others that can be placed into us.

Huxley
This operation he's proposing is insane…yes?
But has the world been waiting for this opportunity…
Have we wanted this all along?
Has it come to this?

That we have become so accustomed to walking the precipice, looking over the edge no longer means anything? Must we fling ourselves from the ledge, just to feel again?
That night in the desert…
Who did we invite through the door?

Filling ourselves to the brim, when what we needed was to be empty.
To be alive but to become the dead.

The General may be much more right than I give him credit for, though perhaps only by coincidence. But despite my position, I know nothing...can our world even be saved? Messages from a nobody are pushing us off the precipice.

We are only acting on the instructions of our ghosts.

Well, enough solitude...send James in here, please.

Belmont
Evening, Sir.

Huxley
Come in James, have a seat. Can I get you anything?
It's been quite a day.

Belmont
I can get it myself, Sir.

Huxley
Nonsense, James. I'm not the President right now. Let me get you a drink.

Belmont
That would be great. I'll take anything right now.

Huxley
Sorry, force of habit...I suppose there isn't much to cheers this evening.

Belmont
Indeed not.
Where are you at with this?

Huxley

That is exactly what I brought you in here to ask. What are your thoughts...beyond that you think they are insane. Do they have a point?

Belmont

That's not the right question to ask.

Because the answer is yes, they have a point, and, yes, they are insane. Anyone can propose a plan at a vulnerable moment, when the world is ready to light a suicidal fuse...and yes, it will always sound like a good plan, when your only tether is unraveling whilst you dangle over the edge, looking death in its grey eyes. Any option that isn't succumbing to that fate, is a good option.

The question isn't are they right, or do they have a point, rather, is what they proposed, avoidable?

Huxley

It'll take a miracle of diplomacy and persuasion to convince the public...or whatever...this is...that there is any other solution. It's like they want it to happen. And I don't just mean those three...you get the sense that everyone wants this?

Belmont

I do...

Within the tragedy is how we can reclaim our identity.

Huxley

That's what I'm afraid of! I mean look at this...

This time even the hippies want the bomb!

Convince me James...Can we find a solution?

Belmont

We as a species have been faced with doomsday's before.

Yet here we are.

Huxley
But what of the mountains of dead it will cause, James.
What of our past days? Where are our better angels?
Where have they gone?
We will have to face the dead someday! What will we say to them?

Belmont
That we never forgot their sacrifice...that they are always with us.

Huxley
Oh bullshit, James!
We don't know anymore. We've forgotten how to live.
It's like we're already dead.

Tell me what you really think.

Belmont
I think you're being a short-sided fool.

No one said this would be easy.
Letting this get to the point of mutual assured destruction is taking the easy path; the path of extremes.

You always told me the easy way is for cowards. So, don't be a coward! Our suffering is getting the best of us.

You're our President...be better than the rest of us!

Huxley
This is far more complex than that, James!

Belmont
No, it isn't.
Whatever this is…is simple.
You either kill millions of people and start a clock of slow and painful extinction…or you don't.

II.IV

Narrator

A limpid dawn, in a world stretched to its limit, and having little chance of escaping itself, begins in horrible silence, like in a fight with a long-time love, that has a serene break. The silence that is louder than the shouted poison; the moment that you realize you've been wrong the whole time, and you are ready to cry from shame, but cannot, because that pause, that serene break, is, as this silent dawn is, scorching away all ability to reason. You hold no words, no thoughts, you are blank, and the dawn rises, and for the briefest, takes over and fills us with much needed emptiness. That dawn, now rises between the buildings of crammed and increasingly neurotic cities, illuminating thousands of tents erected by people who have been waiting their whole life for a moment like this; to be alive, to be filled with purpose, to be finally living with the realization that they may in fact die. The outward escape from everything known previous, into a new reality of only a few days. Inexperienced at knowing their new perfectly alive selves, what mistakes could be made? What would it take to turn a newly generated group into their old selves?

Chorus

Over our time here and all those times we left and returned

The things we create, their visible traces unremarked and
unlearned
We know that to build you need to fasten.
Too often the intermediary between things, is an act that is
hastened
With minimal effort, and carelessness, it fades and falls apart
Likewise, the screw turned too far; the material, like the spirit
does depart.

Narrator
Innocent mistakes are usually the catalysts for most happenings.
And they are more often than not, called innocent mistakes,
when an event's enactment is perpetrated by someone stupid.
The terrible coincidences that bring upon a particular
armageddon, usually by a convenient idiot, or a well-meaning
person not paying attention, which may be the same thing.
History and its particular authors get to make that decision.
They are not however usually present to record a mistaken
sight, thinking that something is; is not. Mistakes that every
rational and intelligent person makes day in and day out,
however, usually without the dominoes of the compendiums of
our discoveries and introspections, placed upright, and ready to
be struck down by a singular misconception.

A bright and refracting light of a serene dawn, a sensuous break
in the fracturing stress, thought to be something more sinister,
more malicious and foreboding, but rather than an omen, it is
simple. A rising sun on the skin of people learning how to live.
A subtle momentary joy. A pure breath to be thieved away by a
convenient idiot.

Silence temporarily lasting through. Silence temporarily
prevailing, seeming as if it will win the day. But minds are
changed in seemingly unmeasurable amounts of time. One
misconceiving mind, spills into another, and another, and

another. The silence that joyously was in each person now learning how to live, was not silence at all, but just a muffling of ears, a loss of sense before tragedy; a deafness – deafness that is shattered back into clear and fluent hearing by a sheet of glass losing its fight against a rock. One sheet of glass, and one rock, then another, and another, and another.

Chorus
When you have forgotten how to live, and the chance to you is given
It takes a wisp of nothing for the people to fall, and all they've built; their constructed heavens.
When cities, and towns, and hamlets fall,
Dumbfounded the gaze and a 'what is it all for' trial.
Our deepest internal questions
Only answered with trigger and clenched fist
The angels and the demons of dual natures it does enlist
The whole-while we build, within our creations; a separate us
Implanting the faulty nail, the weak board, and the rotting truss
To remind us that everything passes, and always must.

Huxley
A digital spirit…a technological magician has taken the whole world hostage! It's time to end this. General, begin the preparations for Operation Dewdrop.

Belmont, Major Mills, Dr. Palmer
No! Please, if you just….

Huxley
Generals…
You know what to do.

PART TWO

ACT III

III.I

Narrator

The artificially illuminated night is no more. A pinnacle of ingenuity and contempt for the natural clocks, the sun's light gives way to a new moon's dark. The people of the tents, wanting to live truly, are now rebound concretely to the cycles of planetary motions, and the risings and settings of light and dark, that only a few yesterdays back, was normalcy for everyone that ever was. But the reality of these days and nights was not in nature itself, but a decision made, at a desk, in an office, signed and co-signed, and witnessed, and stamped, for the protection of a country's people. Filed with a serial number in a cabinet no one is ever going to reference, or be able to find. 'What the people don't know won't hurt them', it was thought, or rather, 'let them have their natural day and their natural night, let them be their new selves; it won't last long. Whomever remains will need this training for the endless winter'. For now, the cities are broken, and lay in darkness. A darkness of protection. For in not seeing the physical world, you cannot harm it. You cannot harm it because you cannot travel to it, without also returning harm in equal proportion upon yourself, or an even greater harm upon yourself, yielding an embarrassing result; the antagonistic warrior vanquished upon his own sword, in idiotic hubris. So the lights are extinguished, and it is hoped for the best, in the darkness and the silence, because the sun will rise again, exposing your position on the battlefield.

But this time, nothing happened. Another day. The sun goes down into another act of darkness. Another act of waiting in fear and introspection, amongst the low-burning fires, and the glass, broken and threatening, on its way back to sand. And that sand, is transformed again into the mortar in between the bricks that one by one protect the objects we cannot live without, because they defined our existences before we did. The great objects and images manifest in the transcendence of a subconscious, married to the motions of hands, are being walled-off. Protecting the building of the protected, from ourselves. Brick by brick, hoping and praying that it will hold, first against the rumble, then against the shockwaves, then against the incessant fire. And when all of that has died down, hoping the bricks hold against an anxious and newly unbalanced us.

Workmen troweling the sand and laying each brick contemplate aloud...

Uffizi Worker I
[12]Quando impareremo?

Uffizi Worker II
Una volta non è bastata?

---

[12] (Italian) When will we learn?

Wasn't once enough?

Who have we become?

Uffizi Worker III
Chi siamo diventati?

Narrator
The saddened guards weeping as they carry treasures.

Uffizi Worker I
[13]Portiamo questo ai sotterranei.
Non che ci possa servire…

Narrator
The usually unregarded, and now invaluable workers, who for the smallest monies, have unending access to what we pay great amounts to see for seconds, hoping for life-changing enlightenment; and they, being wiser than most, know their stipend is to spend the work-a-day life with our greatest treasures, not chasing after what does not need to be chased, look penetratively at these great works.

Weeping collectively, they speak directly to the face of La Primavera.[14]

Uffizi Worker I
[15]Fermati un attimo a guardarlo. Guardalo.

---

[13] This one, to the levels below.
Not that it may do any good…

[14] *Painting by Sandro Botticelli; 1470's - early 1480's*

[15] Take a moment with it. Just look at it.

Uffizi Worker II
[16]Le cose che facciamo per ferirci a vicenda…

Uffizi Worker III
Non impareremo mai?

Uffizi Worker I
Tutte queste opere… tutta questa sapienza…
La nostra emersione dalle tenebre alla luce.
Se non possiamo neanche vedere ciò che ci è davanti,
A cosa è servito tutto questo?

Uffizi Worker I
È come se nessuno ti avesse mai guardato…
Adesso quella cecità volontaria è diventata la nostra morte.

---

[16] The things we do to each other…

Will we never learn?

All of these works…all of this knowledge…
Our emergence from the dark into the light.
If we can't even see what is in front of our faces,
What was it all for?

It is, as if no one even took the time to look at you…
That voluntary blindness is now become our death.

III.II

Narrator

Chipped and weathered game tiles, experientially tossed around on a table, ticking against one another while withered and hard-worked sinewy hands flash back and forth, never touching, always aware; a ballet of perfection from a lifetime in training; sliding and slapping down; usurping tiles and paper and coins in friendly ferocity; the occasional maniacal laughter after a successful and monetarily awarded move. Pale green bottles with equidistant parallel sanded lines atop and bottom, with withered labels, clank constantly. Chair legs and rubber sandaled feet drag and push around dust. Life in an open, sweaty, and dirt-brown palm-green street. The day's joy is broken, as it always is, by the vulgar sound of carefully orchestrated television news; reported seriously and dramatically to people who have known too much, and do not very well need to be told what lies ahead. So, the old continue to play, and let the young worry.

Bar Patron I

[17]Chúng ta phải làm gì đây?

Chúng tôi sẽ không bao giờ thoát khỏi cuộc chiến này...

---

[17] (Vietnamese) What do we do?

We'll never escape this...

Bar Patron II
Có khi không được quan tâm tới như bây giờ lại tốt hơn
Họ không để ý đến chúng tôi.
Nên sẽ chẳng có gì xấu xảy ra.
Ít nhất nó sẽ không xảy ra với chúng tôi.

Bar Patron III
Đó là những gì anh nghĩ thôi, bởi vì anh còn quá trẻ để biết.
Còn tôi thì quá già để có thể quên những gì đã xảy ra.

Bar Patron IV
Chiến tranh, nó đã xảy ra trong quá khứ
Nó sẽ xảy ra lần nữa
Nó luôn xảy đến với chúng tôi.

Bar Patron III
Không ai có thể thoát khỏi cuộc chiến .
Nhưng khi mà ta sống trong một cuộc sống hằng ngày như bị
cầm tù, ta như thể sẽ cảm nhận được sự đa chiều của cuộc

It is nice sometimes, to be unregarded.
They don't care about us.
Nothing will happen.
At least, not to us.

That is what you think, because you are too young to know.
And I am too old to not remember.

It happened before
It will happen again
It always happens to us.

No one is free from this.
But when you are in a constant prison, you see the multidimensionality of
life. And in a way, you are free.

sống này
Và theo một cách nào đó, ta như được tự do.

Bar Patron I
[18]Tất cả chúng ta rồi sẽ là những người thua cuộc.
Rồi sẽ chẳng còn ai sống sót.

Bar Patron IV
Chúng ta cuối cùng rồi sẽ bị xoá sổ khỏi lịch sử loài người.
Ngay cả tổ tiên của chúng ta, những người đã mất, cũng sẽ bị
xoá hết mọi dấu vết.

Bar Patron III
Tất cả rồi sẽ đến hồi kết.
Nên có lo lắng cũng sẽ chẳng giúp gì đâu.

---

[18] We all lose.
No one will remain.

They will have finally, once and for all, struck our history from the
record. Even our dead will die.

It will simply end.
So, there is no need to worry.

III.III

Narrator

An increasingly nervous and unconfident president, paces amongst sculptures of our most highly regarded ghosts; their stone faces with penetrating gazes looking ever downward, locked into a singularly eternal stare. Huxley, affixed into his own mind, and aware neither of his eyes, nor the statues' eyes, breaks his habit and looks up, for an answer from the sky, where we all look to, in times of enigma. The sculptures stare directly at him, but in his mindlessness, and not noticing their time-arrested gaze, Huxley looks straight through them, and their grey-stone, mossy eyes, focusing instead upon the stars; their light dedicated and pointedly beaming down, hitting the stone ghosts, and illuminating the past. Huxley inhales his first cleansing breath in ages, and looking upward into the stone, he begins now to see. The figures have been seeing since the day a chisel bore them eyes, though they were also born lips, they have never spoken. But a sky with only the light from stars can do astounding and unfathomable things.

Huxley

Against all odds…
To exist at all!
But something made it so.
That we even made it this far,

When we shouldn't have had the chance.
And our gifted chance, we gambled,
We, all, petulant adolescents, foolish braggarts of our enlightenments, all so we could avoid the destructive pains of growth.
We voluntarily put a noose around our neck,
Willingly tightening it,
Choking ourselves…
Only to deter another from doing it to us.

How have we approached such a magnanimous emptiness?

It happened so fast,
We haven't had the time yet, to be astonished.

Where are you in all this?
Why build, if only to see creations deliberately destroy themselves! To know that enigmatic mind is exactly what I need right now.

Please! Please answer!

…no I'm not holding my breath…

I must make the decision.
It falls upon my shoulders.
Yes, it is upon my shoulders.

No, no, no, no, no!
Please intervene and stop this insanity!
I can't do this!

There isn't a person alive or dead who knows the answer. No! I cannot handle this situation…No person is cut out for this office. There's no such thing as a knowing ruler…just lucky and unlucky ones. No amount of wisdom is enough for this office.

There are no candles lit.
I am just stammering through the cold and the dark.

Is this really our life?
Surely this is just another dream?
Another raft upon the sea?

If you answered me would I even understand your language?

My decision could be the end of everything…
…how could this come down to just me?
…how did we get here?
…who invented this ridiculous game?

Chorus/Statues
We Did!

Huxley
You!?
Why would you do such a thing?

Chorus/Statues
The same reason you could not help but to play the game.

Huxley
What reason is that?

Chorus/Statues
To vanquish death.
We Vanquished death

We were immortal.
We lived forever,
Now the dead may die
Erased forever.

Huxley
It's not my doing
It was a ghost
Within a machine

It's not my fault
It's not my doing
Preserving life, histories, identities, I swore to do this,
How did I get here!

Chorus/Statues	*Huxley*
We Vanquished death	It's not my doing
We were immortal.	It was a ghost
We lived forever,	Within the machine
Now the dead may die	I swore preservation
Erased forever.	How did I get here!

Narrator
The statues revert to their originally stoic state upon their plinths. And Huxley breathes anxiously, not knowing if what he just saw was real, or simply a hallucinatory manifestation of a heavy burden upon his shoulders, and hoping desperately, that no one saw this, particularly if it were that the sculptures never spoke, or moved, as then he would be writ in the scrupulous and unforgiving annals of history as a leader presented with a great enigma, who within seconds, cracked; so, he resumes his best impression of his usual self, like one does in horrifically embarrassing moments, when you are, for instance, the cause of conversation to come to an expressionistic halt. But here in the garden, there was nothing that the man or the machine

would be able to report upon to a gossamer public. It was just history; the stone book in-the-round, and me, he insisted to himself. His disbelief flowing like a poison into each and every vein; taking every possible pathway, towards a heart, looking to complete its essential duty, overtakes him. He feels the serene break in the fight, an arising dawn, filling him with the emptiness, and there in that silence, an abysmal silence where words never existed, and sound is no such thing, Huxley touches history, with its cool, sometimes smooth, sometimes gritty stone skin. But stone-skin worn by the rain and air, and time, erodes in definitive grit beneath his hands as he touches the stoic past, to ensure that it is no longer alive, and to ensure that he is in fact alive. From one work to another, and another, throughout a meandering maze of cool, weathered stones; keeping no track of where he is, or where he is going, squeezing himself between statues that have the smallest amount of space between them. Studying them and remembering, long-lost college lectures about some of them, why they were important; facts that are not easily remembered by him in this moment, but knows to be true, and these remembrances keep that flame flickering, just low enough to preserve their memory in the category of, for the time-being; immortal. But now, regardless of who they are, what they did, or the help that they could lend him in the greatest of moments; this moment, Huxley is blank, blissfully closed off from the past, and its intrinsic gravity upon the present. He breathes again, and after a deep inhalation, Huxley doesn't simply see them as stones; but sees into their eyes. Eyes that are lit only by the stars. Despite the peaceful and transcendent moment, it remains forcibly dark, because the decision was made that advertising himself with unnecessary light, could be his end; an existence the emperor now shares with the plebeians.

No longer used to darkness, unguarded, vulnerable, and overtaken by the intoxication of disbelief, Huxley blithely meanders alone. An action that he has forgotten as a man of his office tends to. But like all wandering as well as purposeful things, there is an end. But some ends are beginnings, such as his approachment to an old door, and realizing he's never noticed it previously, for when you hold this office, walks in your own garden, are like walking new paths; it was always there, but you never had the time, or took the steps for yourself. This door, emitting the stale air of something that wanted to, but had not breathed in some time, is ajar just enough to illicit the curiosity and anxiety inherent to everyone. The riveted, grey metal, that once was impenetrable and now rusting, is calling Huxley, which is to say, he is looking for any escape from the current unanswerable enigma that no person in any office, in any world, could answer correctly. This is his out. He knows it. He does not question it.

Finagling his way with as much confidence as anyone who happens upon an aged, tarnished metallic door they have never seen, and is looking for an escape from a horrifically unanswerable situation can muster, trepidatiously steps through. After seconds that seem like cold, silent minutes, the door slowly shrieking and scraping, closes behind him. He looks back and with what little light exists he sees a wheel in the center of the door. The door closes, with a finality that makes one naturally, think of their end, a thing they thought would come at a later time, and when that inner darkness settles, and he regains calmness, the wheel turns with a sharper degree of finality, exposing only a narrow claustrophobic path. It seems his only way. What choice does he have? The wheel has turned. The light, perhaps some of the last artificial light on the planet, decrescendos to a point, a beacon of pure blackness. There is nothing to do but walk. The clip-clop of his presidential shoes strike against the hard floor in regimented time signature, the steps towards the blackness, an emptiness that becomes greater, a blackness painted with bigger and wider brush strokes, abruptly stops. And with all things that stop that instantaneously, it gives way to something that begins in at least equal or sometimes even greater initiation. His void, shattered by a single pinpoint of light, a singular star in a black sky. And in this particular abstruse world, previously unseen to President Huxley, though in constant proximity to him, another pinpoint of light appears. And then another. So that the blackness is no more, and the lights exponentiating in their births, blink at him, as if he is a light also unto them. They are alive, moving, blinking; a nighttime of star eyes, watching and guiding. Something in his first years, perhaps, he dreamed, as alike things we all imagined before our great age of reason thieves its way into our existences. Forgetting that, or willingly tossing it away, and with the exuberance of a child not able to differentiate actuality from dream, his path now lit, Huxley walks with a new confidence, a renewed purpose, making time seemingly speed up, and his night of syncopatedly blinking eye-stars gives way to a dawn. And in that dawn, he is faced with another, once impenetrable door, riveted, and rusting. A wheel at its center, and upon each clock-point, a hand. Considering the nature of the eyes in the gauntlet, he assumes these hands also are real. Touching one gingerly, to test his assumption it slightly and shamefully moves. This he knows is the only way out of the gauntlet, a gauntlet he made peace with, but a place which no one would intend to stay. Knowing he has to leave, he inhales a breath of confidence, not real confidence of course, but a confidence of superficiality, because topical artifice is the way that real-life situations are approached by politicians, which is to say, those who have not attended the school of life, must present a façade of understanding the sufferance of the common. There is no time for timidness. He chooses one of the dozen hands on the wheel, breathes deep, and grasps it. The wheel-hand not having felt another's touch in an amount of time no one is sure of, grasps his hand with force, like someone desperately yearning for touch, multiplied by a complete lack of social grace; the wheel holds his hand and does not release. In the natural panic that occurs from something unfathomable, yet nevertheless very real, he unknowingly and mistakenly lets his free hand get grasped by another hand of the wheel; like children getting the ball stuck in the tree, that was used to release the previous ball. And in the struggle, he remembers the confidence gained while in the gauntlet, the superficial breath, the artificial courage, and plays this card again. The fight dwindles. Hands still imprisoned in one another the wheel begins to turn. One half-turn of the wheel and the bodiless hands release Huxley's. One last clip-clop through the door and his next steps are onto sand. He stops after his first few, realizing the absurdity of such a pair of shoes, and looking up he sees that his gauntlet has opened into another, one with more air and immeasurable openness, but such an openness as to be useless to any man, empty space, that will only swallow you, so expansive as to be closed-off, a thing that exists, but perhaps shouldn't; the only positive space, a very small isthmus of beach with a pigeon-grey ocean surrounding, and the sound of two scavenger birds, and a benign wind. The isthmus comes to a sharp and precarious point, and it is as if Huxley is walking upon the flat face of a swords' blade, and at its point is a raft, something he knows, but cannot specifically remember where from. It is an object most are no longer used to seeing, a hand-carved object of necessity, for a bygone people. Embellished with scenes of a particular history, and images that as Huxley inspects, he is not sure if they are only historic, or are representations of what is yet to come as well. It is intricate and esoteric, written in a language we all spoke, but at another time, a time of more pragmatic and purposeful connectivity. Just the same as he knows the raft, but cannot remember from where, he knows the birds. Black, glossy, and attentive, almost as if waiting for him, but for what purpose? He knows they will stay with him, even remembers them, and they him. That much was internally evident, when they saw each other. To ward off disbelief and ensure a reality of some sort, enough tactility to concretely convey that this is not a dream; that I am here, this is happening, and I am real, and so is this raft, as are these loyal, black, and glossy birds; and like the sculptures in his garden, he runs his hands over the raft. This is real. Taking one last examining look at its carved and painted images, he sees something he remembers. A design of tight, simple lines carved into the wood. Huxley now remembers, something. A fragment, that in itself is undefined, but it is enough to instill some sort of confidence, he knows where he is going, he knows how to get there. Pushing off what little of the raft is touching the isthmus, and jumping on just as the last portion relinquishes the ground; he is out to sea. But unceremoniously, and at a disappointingly short distance from the isthmus' tip, the raft comes to a gentle halt. The deafening silence of unfulfilled anticipation is broken, as the raft, slowly begins to sink, flatly and evenly, something that should not happen; the birds caw, then leave. Huxley's feet without binds are cemented to the raft's floor, and he remembers the power of calmness. Placing a hand on his chest, and inhaling the depth of breath one must take when knowing submergence in water is inevitable, a breath so large because you think it may be your last; he and the raft go down below the surface. His feet never becoming unstuck. But all ends have new beginnings.

III.IV

Narrator
Traveling through time and purposeful dreaming is not a luxury given to people that are particularly noble, or wise; but rather it is a necessity of all people desiring to know, the most efficacious path towards a useful future. Without that travel, making the right decision about anything is wishful guessing. When we travel in time, it is always right.

Huxley
How long has it been?

Thucydides
Too long, my friend. Too long!
Time moves fast, and it moves slowly. It is everything and it is nothing.

But that is no matter right now. We can discuss this and more over dinner. I have invited some friends to join. They are awaiting us, now. And I assume you came here again, to discuss some very pressing matters?

Huxley
I did indeed!

Thucydides
Then let's go and clear our minds!

Narrator
They walk and share the banter of long-time friends; down the dusty and fertile roads, of an ancient age, eventually arriving to Thucydides' house where others await their arrival.

Democritus
Greeting my friend! So...I understand your world is about to end?

Huxley
Ahh...?

Democritus
You must be quite nervous.

Huxley
Wouldn't you be!

Democritus
I don't know. I have never been in that position before.
I try not to get too nervous about things, you know?
Worlds begin and end all the time.
This wouldn't be the first time...nor the last.

Huxley
I have people to protect, morals and values to uphold.
Worlds have not ended by such horrific methods as this!

Zeno
That you know of.

Huxley
I suppose that is not untrue.
But I must preserve what is in my grasp, rather than let the whims of a universe have its way with me...wait...what do you mean that you know of?

Zeno
The way I understand it, it's not the universe having its way with you...it's people. People warped and twisted, by unchecked fear.

Huxley
Ok...Yes.

Democritus
Well that's a big difference.
Also...morals and values?
Killing to live...nothing moralistic about that.

Huxley
But what you must understand...

Democritus
Tut, tut. Trust me.

Huxley
But what do you mean that you know of?

Thucydides
Do you know that this method of destruction hasn't existed before?

Ask yourself...how many times have we been here? How many worlds have there been?

Huxley
You mean to say that we've been here before?
On the edge of this very precipice?

Thucydides
I know it seems dark but realize there are many middle paths.
Even when it seems too dark to see, they are there.
You are also a victim of the same fear that is driving your world.
You are not a god.

Zeno
The generals that are scraping at your bones, are not gods either.

Thucydides
People are driven to believe whatever narrative they invent to
get what they want.
Someone to place the blame on, when it all goes awry.

Democritus
They're only chasing this path because if they don't, they think
another will do it to them...self-preservation...what a waste of
time.

Thucydides
In our time, the gods were there to take the blame away from
us.
But we did this.
All of us.
Forever and ever.
In our day and yours.

Huxley
Why do you always come to me?

Thucydides
It has always been the other way around, my friend.

Huxley
I suppose it is that I need to convene with history.
I cannot trust the living

Zeno
But we are all very much alive.

Thucydides
We've been here before, perhaps we'll be back around again.
Suffering comes in enough forms; you needn't invent new ones.
You'll need a clear mind.
Take this...

Huxley
What is this?

Democritus
A truly magnificent potion. It will help you clearly see the answers you seek. Your eyes will penetrate the layers of time, and it will open your mind to infinite possibilities. You will travel anywhere in space that you desire, unlocking all paradoxes.

Huxley
Ok...here we go.
Nothing happened.

This just tastes like wine...

Thucydides, Democritus, Zeno
Ha Ha Ha!!!

Democritus
There's your magic potion, son!

Huxley
Thank you, but the situation at hand is...

Democritus
Oh, right. Your world is about to end.

Thucydides
You're worried that you've all come too close to the edge, yes?
That a tiny something, a benign occurrence, will send you plummeting downwards, yes?
This is hardly new.

Huxley
But weapons of such magnificent destruction as these!

Zeno
This is also hardly a new thing.
Isn't their power a blessing?

Huxley
How could it be a blessing?

Democritus
I told you to leave morality out of this.

Huxley
I didn't just now mention, morality.

Thucydides
You're at the precipice of war are you not?
What got you there?

Huxley
There was a man, or a machine, or…

Thucydides
No. That is what pushed you over.
What got everyone to that edge?

Huxley
Blind interest and unchecked fear, I suppose.

Thucydides
Fear of what?

Huxley
Ah, um, well…it was, well…

Thucydides
Fear that one cannot exist, while does the other.
Tell me, is your world only filled with one kind of people?

Huxley
Well…no…but what does that have to do with morality?

Democritus
The whole goddamn thing is immoral! You're planning to go to war! You say you have morals and values to protect…you can be rest assured, that the other side is justifying their next move by the same nonsense…That somehow, they cannot survive while you do.

Zeno
You have sustained yourselves well.
You all live, simultaneously…yet you think you cannot.
Obsessing about the future, while being completely blind to your present.

Thucydides
Making it impossible to understand the past.
Enough for now...let's eat...you need a clear mind.

DINNER

Huxley
That was wonderful.

Thucydides
You must certainly be feeling better now.

Huxley
I am still wracked by my present conundrum.
If we don't kill them, they will probably kill us…

Democritus
What are you, six?

Thucydides
So certain the middle path is gone?

Huxley
It is gone.

Zeno
You are so quick to plant your flag and imprison yourselves…all of you!

Democritus
Indeed.
You are not fighting between nations…
Your whole world is attempting a personal prison break!
You want to do the right thing, Hux? Ask yourself, who you are. Are you free? Or your own prisoner? Whose shackles do you hope to break?

Thucydides
And with that, we drink to you breaking the whole world out of their prison!

Thucydides, Democritus, Zeno
To Huxley !

Narrator
Clearing their minds, the impromptu symposium transitions to further and increasingly less coherent conversation, and a game of kottabos.

Democritus
Tell me Hux, do you believe in an endless string of worlds beyond worlds, and infinite lives?

Huxley
Goodness, yes! I have so far lived three times!

Democritus
You've lived three times…You needn't our advice, we should be seeking your counsel!

Narrator
Huxley's wine-lee strikes the saucer, releasing it, and falling to the base of the stand, striking the bell.

Thucydides
Ho!

Zeno
He got that one!

Thucydides, Democritus, Zeno
Fill the pitcher
Fill the saucer
Slam it down, and then another!
Our man Huxley
Lived three lives

With more to spare
Might as well make it another!

Narrator
Downing saucer upon saucer, they make it another, and then another. Huxley's mind, now clear with the magic potion required for major decision-making, and in the short-lived good graces of what little delicate space lies between the moment of the potions' advantageous apex and its declination towards it all being a nauseous waste of time, he decides to retire for the evening.

Huxley
I've got a lot to think about. I am away!

Zeno
Good night

Democritus
Go save the world, Hux!

Thucydides
Good night my friend.

Narrator
Huxley meanders down a hallway with numerous identically heavy wooden doors, unsuccessfully trying several of them, until finally on the fourth, or maybe seventh try, a door opens, and he slips through with unexpected speed, due to his misunderstanding of weights and measures that are innate to most; as they are him, just not at this particular point in time. Furniture being knocked over and scrawled against a stone floor echoes through the cold hallways. Miraculously coming to an understanding, or, an involuntary but mutually agreeable relationship with physics, he awards the house of Thucydides,

with silence. Until the door, like many of the objects Huxley encountered in the room, shatters the silence as it is slammed shut. The thick weathered wood meets the stone jamb violently, reverberating the sound of drunkenness throughout the hallways.

III.V

Narrator

Footsteps tramp upon an autumnal forest floor, there is no light present, it is black; not because that is what is there, but because that is what Huxley sees, or does not see, and then the footsteps stop, and when constant rhythm is broken there is always the suspenseful silence, because something has to come next, but we do not know what. The anodyne sound of a light turning on, the drawn-out slow snap of a lamp's pull-chain. The sound has happened, but the light has not broken. In the darkness, Huxley internally panics: 'I heard the lamp turn on, but I cannot see; am I blind? Is this a dream? It must be, because a light has been illuminated; I know the sound; but I cannot see, and that was not so when I went to bed, so it must be a dream. Yes? The light will present itself; I am not blind.' And the light does present itself. And when he begins to see, he also tastes, the dampness of leaves on the ground; the same leaves that were being crunched by footsteps that surely were not his. Coming into first foggy, and then lucently clear-focus, there is a table, and on that table, there is the lamp with the pull-chain, and green glass shade, vibrantly lit. Two cups of pitch-black coffee, resting on bone-white saucers upon the table, and awaiting his company is himself.

The Huxley of the Forest
He awakes!

Huxley
Indeed, I have.
I see I am present with…myself.
Dead or alive?

Narrator
Huxley tests his own question by picking up a sharpened stone upon the table, placed there presumably for this assurance of existence, a stone that was purposely carved, in a bygone era, by its aesthetic. Holding out his hand in an apprehensive and sacrificial manner, he runs the stone blade across his index finger; he bleeds.

Huxley
Alive still!

The Huxley of the Forest
Still…or again?
Come…join me.

Huxley
Again?

The Huxley of the Forest
Do you know where we are?

Huxley
No.

The Huxley of the Forest
But you do in fact know, don't you?

Huxley
I have been here before, haven't I?

The Huxley of the Forest
You tell me.
Come up here, have some coffee.

Huxley
Thank you. That is exactly what I need.

Narrator
Huxley takes a long pensive look at the coffee. It looks and smells like his cups that serve as the brief gift during his stressful presidential days. He sips. It is as delicious as he hoped, warming and bitter. But when placing the cup down upon the saucer, with shaking hands from the nervousness of having coffee with himself, some spills out, filling the indentation of the saucer. He knows all too well that when the gravity of the cup interrupts this pool, it shoots out everywhere, creating an uncomfortable abstraction to the perfection and cleanliness of the cup's previously pristine state. Huxley is greatly perturbed by this unwanted abstraction, in a world he does not know, and is trying his best to navigate.

Huxley
The perfection ruined.

The Huxley of the Forest
Allow me. It is no matter.
Always more perturbance and stains, where we usually don't look.
Strive for perfection, yes, but do not suffer for it.
You seem nervous? There is no need.
You are here with yourself, the one you know best.

Huxley
No one knows themselves.
But strangely I know this place.

The Huxley of the Forest
What do you know about it?

Huxley
Only that I have been here before…perhaps a thousand times.

The Huxley of the Forest
What else?

Narrator
Huxley the original, gets up from the chair and paces the forest. He picks up leaves, crunches them in his hands, for no particular reason other than to hear the sound, and feel the whole form with minimal effort turn to a dust.

Huxley
This is the situation I am in.

Narrator
Continuing to pace and not answer his copy's original question, he picks up a stick and plays for a moment like a little boy with a sword; storming a castle, or jumping from one ship to the next. His adulthood taking hold, he stops playing to think about the question just asked of him.

Huxley
The air.
I have breathed it before,
It is same air breathed by my ancestors.
And I breathe the air for those yet to come,
I've spent aeons here.

But I dismissed it.
Waved it away like a childish thing, thinking I had grown.
It became unnecessary, disposable.

Narrator
Still holding the stick, his swordplay becomes more serious,
tactical and practiced; someone who has studied the art-form.

Huxley
I was acting as an adult...when I should have been as a child.
Something that has never known war.

This is where we begin, isn't it?
Why did I dismiss it?

Narrator
The Huxley of the Forest pours two fresh cups of coffee.

The Huxley of the Forest
Because you had to.
All people must.
You cannot stay.
Many try, but it will reject you.
If you cling to it, it will tear, and the harder you grasp the
quicker it becomes the dried leaves turned to dust in your hand.
Those that cling to parents, no matter how long, will someday
find themselves alone. It is in the world, as it is in these woods.

Huxley
I didn't leave, I was rejected.

The Huxley of the Forest
Yes. Everyone is at some point.
These woods are a place of beginnings. Not of endings.
Consciousness is lighted here.

But there is more than just consciousness.
You know this.

Huxley
What came before these woods?

The Huxley of the Forest
Everything.
But after these woods, you live only a few seconds.
Almost nothing.

Huxley
A few seconds?

The Huxley of the Forest
Seems impossible, yes?

Huxley
Not impossible…just…discouraging.

The Huxley of the Forest
Yes, well...
Let's walk. There is something you need to see.

Huxley
You are going to take me to the edge of the woods.

The Huxley of the Forest
You are indeed astute.
I am.
You cannot stay.

Huxley
I am being rejected. By myself!

The Huxley of the Forest
You were already rejected.
There is something else for you this time around.

Narrator
Huxley and The Huxley of the Forest begin to walk. They are in discussion about everything and nothing; the woods illicit conversation we never knew we possessed. In them, we are wiser than we were so previously. The forest is a great teacher of things we already know.

The two reach the tree line, beyond which, barely visible, is a field and a gravely road. In the woods, contrary to what should be, is the light of day. Beyond the line, contrary to what should be, is the stark contrast of a night lit only by stars and a singular, distant fire.

The Huxley of the Forest
I cannot go with you.
This is your path.
The end of your beginning.
You will know what to do.

Huxley
What is that light on the horizon?

The Huxley of the Forest
Go to it. You will know it when you see it.
You've been there before.

III.VI

Huxley
Hello.

Tautamata
Hello.
You seem as though you don't know where you are, but that isn't true is it? You know exactly where you are...You have been here before.

Huxley
More than once. But this time is different...a new reason that I'm here...yes...I have been here before...but I haven't the time for bygone things.

Tautamata
It is those bygones in which you know your future.
You must leave...but do not disregard this fire.
You were here before.

More than once.
Remember that.

You are always welcome here, at this fire.

But it is much better for everyone to not come back.

I wonder if I will see you again?

Goodbye.

III.VII

Narrator
Now thoroughly confused, Huxley is left second-guessing
where he has been, and what lives he has lived. He leaves the
fire with more questions than answers, and the light of the fire,
which was bright, only in that it was a singular light, save for
the stars, dwindles into a minuscule point on the horizon. And
on another horizon beyond his own, there is a faint but
recognizable sound; quietly echoing voices of a mass of people.
As he walks the sun rises, as it always will, providing he
remains bold and courageous on his path.

Chorus
Let go the ropes
That hold the curtain

Narrator
A people, visible in the arising sun, proceed down the road in
slow religious rhythm.

Chorus
Looking out
In each direction
The guardians of past and future
Sacrificed upon your altar

Let go the ropes
That hold the curtain
We Vanquished death
We were immortal.
We lived forever,
The dead have died
Erased forever

We Vanquished death
We were immortal
We lived forever

Now the dead have died erased forever!

Narrator
In the habit of his office, prepared speeches are always recalled
from his mind's library, whether made to previous audiences,
or held in preparation for the right moment; either way, making
them truly disingenuous. Huxley, now face-to-face with the
chanting mass, sees they are horrifically wounded and maimed.
No wars he knew of could have caused such catastrophic and
visceral injuries. In the aesthetic horror, he fears he has become
a speechless president; which is to say, completely useless.
Then, he remembers a chapter from the book his friend wrote;
closing his eyes, breathing deep, he improvises to meet the
occasion.

Huxley
Thank you for coming to me today and taking part in
such an important tradition of our collective sacrifice.
Know that though I may not convince in totality, every
word I speak to you today is truth. And in that truth, I
am all too aware of my own imperfections and abilities
to perfectly memorialize sacrifice of such magnitude.

To celebrate our victories and defeats is to celebrate the actions of our ancestors, those who are responsible not only for us in the flesh but also in mind. Our decisions, our actions, thoughts and feelings only are...because theirs were also. We are, because of them, and it is a vacuous discontent, not to truly know those responsible for our breath.

They are us, and we them, but we cannot know them. It is impossible. Though we yearn for them that is not enough, save perhaps in dream, but then is it a phantom, not flesh.

In death is the only way to know our ancestors, and ourselves.

Chorus
We know them!
We are them!

Huxley
Indeed! We continue to reach for them!

Narrator
In automatic reaction, he encourages, gives thumbs-up, and open-palmed signs of calming and resistance. The gestures he is all too used to employing in front of anxious crowds, to quell and maintain control of the story. A story that is not his to tell.

Chorus
We are them!
We know them!
The dead have died erased forever!

Huxley

They are the only efficacious path to our future! And what a path was cut! Our present, is an age of great benefit, and with that comes great anxiety. With blessing must indeed come, curse. Many will tell you that they long for a simpler time, or that it isn't like it used to be; they will say that our era, is being lost by us, or has abandoned us. But it is not so, my friends! All things are an evolution! The proof is us. We are here. And we will continue on forever! Even within the anxiety of our own creations, it is not enough to destroy us completely!

Narrator

An anxious and growing mass, met with more presidential hand- gestures...

Huxley

We have learned so much...yet what we know is so little. The abilities that knowledge affords us comes with great responsibility; responsibility to not let fear of the unknown dictate us or force us into impatient choices; choices of extreme consequence.

Chorus

Can you not see what is in front of you?

Huxley

Although the eyes of an enemy may occasionally profit by the liberality gained from our greatness, they survive only a minute in comparison to our eternity.

Chorus

Your eyes did profit
We knew ourselves

Where we were going
We were not fearful
You took our path and walked it for us…

We vanquished death!
We were immortal!

Huxley
Yes, yes…here, here! And your noble sacrifices, as I witness here and now, the harm brought to you by whatever battles you've just endured, will heal in short course and lead to more prosperous times.

Though these moments are heavy…inscribe them in whatever means will preserve them for yours, and theirs after, as yours did for you. Inscribe it within you, it will flow in your blood, and be present in future blood.

You, their survivors will continue to keep open the curtain.

Chorus
Let go the ropes!

                Let go the ropes!

                                Let go the ropes!

Let go the ropes!

                Let go the ropes!

                                Let go the ropes!

Narrator
The wounded mass produce ropes. They begin tying them into the most malicious and definitive of knots. They are a people,

that can handle no more; like the man or the machine creating a monumentally anxious public, these chanting wounded, are now the deciders of Huxley's fate.

Chorus
We Vanquished death
We were immortal.
We lived forever,
The dead have died
Erased forever

Narrator
The mass begins to encircle Huxley. A rope is placed around his neck.

Huxley
What are you doing!

Chorus
We are only acting on the instructions of our ghosts.

Narrator
Another rope.

Huxley
There is so much work yet to be done!
It is painful now...
But do not let your wounds be in vain!

Narrator
Huxley feels the weight of a third rope. He approaches one of the wounded as true fear begins to sink into his flesh; penetrating to the bone. Huxley touches the peeled flesh of a mother, clinging to an equally harmed and completely innocent child. With no preemption, no noticeable passing of even a

measurable instant of time, he weeps the tears of a man who has begun to understand the multidimensionality of existence; the fruition of decisions upon the lives of people. Those not bred in the captivity which so many are unknowingly accustomed. Huxley then moves to another victim, touches their face and sees the exposed and heat-tarnished skull through burned flesh. Huxley's breath quickens, and his fear is like a virus replicating and maneuvering through his blood at light-speed.

Huxley
Oh God…
Oh God…
No…No!

Narrator
Huxley approaches another. A man whose arms were involuntarily taken, accompanied by a woman; completely burned. Her flesh blackened, other portions are red and glossy with still alive, palpitating viscous blood, and the very unpresidential sound of vomit splatters to the ground; a deep gasping breath, panting and spitting.

Huxley
I didn't mean for…
I had no choice…
We had to get to this point for…for…
What was I supposed to do?
If I didn't do this, they would have…

It would have happened either way!

Chorus
Maybe…

Narrator
Looking Huxley in the eye, with the calmness of a monk, and the emotional indifference of an executioner, two nuclear victims pull tight the nooses around his neck. Huxley, shocked at the lightning-quick tightening of the slipknot, and an immediate loss of breath, reaches out. Tears slowly coming down his cheeks, bile and saliva still coating his lips. He calmly touches their burned faces.

Huxley
I had no choice…
Is there no undoing what I have done!

Narrator
A fourth rope tightens.

Huxley
I had…
I had…
No…choice…

Narrator
The final rope. Placed. Tightened. Gasping. But no air is coming to aid him. In his remaining and rapidly fading consciousness, he feels a trickle down his face. Tears, he assumes. And these tears he concludes is his life being strangled from him, memories escaping and rapidly replaying, taken by those that he knowingly but not-quite voluntarily killed. It was the man, or the machine, and not-quite him, whilst not-not him, he was just the holder of the office. With what translucently remaining consciousness he holds, there is an intrinsic sense, like a person has when inhaling an awakening breath upon a raft of a beginning, that this trickle upon his face flows too fast and plentifully for it to be tears. And with strength mustered through

the uncanny processes of biology we possess when threatened with death, he maneuvers his neck slightly up to the sky; just enough of the sky to see that it is rain, and not his life, and experiences, coming out of him, just yet. A flicker of hope in his impossible situation; a momentary prolongation of life, or, escape from death.

The sea is violent, the raft is a tussled toy upon it, and the victims are unrelenting. Huxley becomes hypoxically calm; not at peace, he is in fact enraged, at the prospect of dying; but he is a man about to enter the same world as those tightening and pulling at the nooses, it cannot be fought against. A few seconds longer, and his breath is no longer diminishing or even fading, but has stopped. The victims relent as their aim has been met.

They let go the ropes.

Dragged to the edge of his raft, with the indifference from his victims as those in the past have had for a captured and tortured dictator, he is rolled into the sea. Ropes still attached to his neck, he sinks into the cold and the dark.

Face down on the stone floor, of his unknowingly chosen chambers in Thucydides' home, he is soaking wet from being thrown into the sea. Huxley runs out the door, with purpose never before felt in his life.

Democritus
What happened to you?
Go for a swim in your dreams?

Huxley
I have to go back! Right away!

Thucydides
You saw something important tonight, didn't you?

Huxley
I need to go back and undo what I've done...or what I could do...

Zeno
So...you are yet to make a mistake? This needs undoing?

Huxley
...Yes?
I began to make a mistake and left the reins to a few who will...well...paint a very ugly future.

Democritus
Are you free now?

Huxley
I broke out of my prison!
I have to go back.
No time to waste.
Come back with me...all of you.
Our world needs you...more than ever!

Narrator
Pouring four saucers of wine, Democritus motions all over to the table. Each takes their saucer and raises it.

Huxley
...we don't have the time for...ok maybe just one...

Democritus
I'm in.

Zeno
As am I.

Thucydides
I would love nothing more.

Huxley
Let's go save ourselves from ourselves!

ACT IV

IV.I

Narrator
The emboldened four, emerge from the same paths previously walked alone by Huxley. The Greeks taking in their new surroundings meander throughout the sculptures in the garden, like graceless tourists in a museum.

Democritus
Well, here you are!

Thucydides
That doesn't look a thing like me…

Zeno
History, and generously unaware sculptors, certainly made you more handsome than you ever were.

Huxley
This way…
Also…I'd be careful what you say to these things…

Zeno
They are stone…

Huxley
They are indeed, and yet I'm telling you…
Just be mindful of what you say around them.

Narrator
The President's office, where the decision to initiate Operation Dewdrop was made, is the same office, now having many more people milling about. More chiefs of things, more tables, more maps, more blinking and beeping monitors with numeric scales, and differently colored lights representing levels or severities of a great many somethings. Officials standing officially and sipping from coffee cups; low-ranking lackeys running around delivering that coffee, and a few elder militarists, swirling courage-lifting snifters. Huxley's office has now changed to an overly crowded office of world domination. The melee of misguided intellectual chess could have been easily, and perhaps more efficaciously completed in the War Room, however, in there is the immovable, and truthfully inconvenient stone book.

Sergeant I
General, the first round of planes has just left the base.
Will be arriving to targets in three hours.

General Mitchell
Thank you, Sergeant.
My child leaves the nest today.
By God, I could cry.

Where are we on communications?

Sergeant II
No one can see us.

General Harris
Don't get too cocky. They know where we are.
Battle is more than the eyes.
Inducing panic, awakens unknown abilities…
There is no protection in our forest.

General White
They won't know anything about anything in three hours.

Major Mills
There are more they's, than you can possibly count.

Lieutenant I
I may have something here.

General Mitchell
Yes?

Lieutenant I
NOAA is reporting aircraft movement in several sectors.

General Mitchell
How can it be?
We have eyes, they do not.

Dr. Palmer
There are more eyes looking at us than we will ever know!

General Mitchell
Shut up.
What about the alternate channels?

Sergeant III
Same.

Colonel Lewis
Our eyes are not working.

General White
We are more blind than we thought.

General Mitchell
No. We just can't see as clearly as we should.
No Matter. This will be over soon enough.

General Harris
Over for who?

General Mitchell
Shut up.
Have the wings report in.

Sergeant I
Yes sir.

Narrator
Encoded calls from radios in the room, are sent and re-sent. Repeated attempts to reach the first barrage of attack planes, yields no positive results. Worry and embarrassment begins to crowd the faces of previously confident generals.

Sergeant III
Nothing Sir.

General Mitchell
What do you mean nothing…how can that possibly be?

Sergeant III
It means, there is an absence of something, sir.

Sergeant I
It is empty...

Sergeant II
There is nothing...

General Mitchell
Nothing?
That is no such a thing.
Keep trying.
We will prevail.
We are doing the right thing.

Narrator
Huxley enters and everyone rises, out of habit, though few consider him the one in power anymore. That fact is written on the faces of even the lower ranking men and women in the room. The Greeks enter swiftly behind him. Their clothing did not change when coming to the present, Huxley's did. An enigma perhaps, of time-travel.

General Mitchell
Mr...President?

Huxley
General...I see you've begun without me.

General Mitchell
Well once again, Sir, if you'll recall you gave me permission to begin this operation. Unsurprisingly you seem to have been absent at a key moment...and I see you've brought some...friends?

Huxley
Advisers...you might say

General Mitchell
Strangely dressed for advisors.

Huxley
General, I am ordering you to cease Operation Dewdrop.

General Mitchell
And did these...um...advisors...tell you to do this?

Huxley
In an indirect way.
It is none of your concern why I decided to call off this operation. Need I remind you...you serve at the pleasure of the president.

General Mitchell
I assure you, sir, these last few days together have not been all that pleasurable.

Thucydides
No matter how much time passes, nothing ever seems to change. Generals...

General Mitchell
I'm sorry, what?
Who are these people?

Huxley
Advisers, I said.

General Mitchell
What do you mean...Generals...?
What would you know about that!

Thucydides
Well... I did used to be one.

Huxley
Call off this operation immediately.

General Mitchell
I can't exactly do that.

Huxley
And why is that?

General Mitchell
As you'll recall...the first step of phase II...sir...is to send planes...beginning preliminary attacks.

Huxley
Yes...?

General Mitchell
And those planes are only two hours from their target.

Huxley
Well that's no matter...just call them back.

General Mitchell
Call them back!
Heh!...
Call them back?
Call...
Well...
Sir...
We have...
Well it's not that easy....
I can't just call them back!

Huxley
Because?

General Mitchell
Well, because...

Sergeants I, II, III
Because he is blind.

General Mitchell
I have eyes!
That being said...it does...however seem.... that we may
have...temporarily...

Huxley
Yes?

General Mitchell
...lost...communication...with them.

Huxley
You are blind then.
You have no eyes or ears...you never did.

Major Mills and Dr. Palmer
There are more eyes upon you than you will ever know.

Huxley
Do everything you can to reclaim your senses, General.
Not just for your sake, for everyone...past, present, and future.
I swore to preserve, and that is exactly what I plan on doing...
With or without you, General!

General Mitchell
We will try, sir.

Huxley
You will do.

Narrator
A dejection coupled with an emasculating silence. The four depart.

General Mitchell
General White, Colonel Lewis…you, you, you, and you…come with me.

IV.II

General Mitchell
What a lunatic! He can't do this to me…to us!
And who the hell were those people?

Lieutenant I
Totally ridiculous, sir. Unbefitting of his office.

General Mitchell
Shut up.
Well…he's obviously lost his mind.
He is no longer fit to rule.

General White
What do you suggest?

General Mitchell
We move forward.
Without eyes.

General White
The excuse of blindness.

| *Sergeant I, II, III* | *Lieutenant I, II, III* |
| Ingenious! | Ingenious! |

General Mitchell and General White
Shut up.

Colonel Lewis
We stay the course?

General Mitchell
Stay the course...
Sergeant can you continue to pretend to attempt contact with those planes?

Sergeant I
I can.

General Mitchell
Lieutenants...can you give a confident performance, in boldly doing a jobless job ?

Lieutenants I, II, III
We can indeed.

Lieutenant I
How is it...that we will confidently do a jobless job?

General Mitchell
Next time you walk around these offices...look at people holding papers...do you know what those papers say...do you care? No! Of course not. Because they are doing a job, yes...so...do that.

The planes will be there in one hour. Once they strike, it is just dominoes.

Our new and better world will be here before we know it. Let's get out there and do nothing!

Oh, and Lieutenant...double security around the operations-center...

Lieutenant I
The President's office, sir?

General Mitchell
Ex-president's office.
He no longer holds any power.
I want it on lock-down.

Lieutenant I
Sir.

IV.III

Belmont
Sir...and...

Huxley
James...we must call this off. It must be stopped, by any and every means possible.

We can still preserve.

Belmont
I agree!
Sir...who...are they?

Huxley
Of all people, I'm surprised to have to tell you.
James, everyone, I'd like to introduce Thucydides, Democritus, and Zeno.

Major Mills
You went back, again...didn't you, sir?
Through the sea...

Huxley
I did, Major. I did.

Belmont
Do you think they bought it?

Huxley
Bought what?

Belmont
It's a wise choice of characters, to be sure…
But do you think they will get the lesson?

Huxley
Lesson? No, no…I brought them…back with me.
To save the world!

Belmont
I'm sorry?
Sir, even I find these actors to be a bit of a stretch.
An excellent effort…creative…and…

Major Mills
Oh, they are very real, Ambassador. Their journey to us, this day, through the sea, and annals of time, is exactly what we need. It was not accidental.

Thucydides
Nice to see you again, Major.

Major Mills
And you, General.

Belmont
Regardless, I'm with you to stop this nonsense.
We can preserve everything.
To never have begun, will be the only thing erased today.

IV.IV

Narrator

Encampments formed, doctrines exposed, and malice's unclothed; the fight for our past, present, and future, has come to President Huxley's office. No person when running for an office of this magnitude, or a person automatically appointed, by virtue of from whom they burst forth, by no choice of their own, is actually ready for this. But it has come. A lack of preparation, will, or courage is not an excuse. Huxley, his bygone, yet fully present ancient friends, and present-day allies walk with great and defined purpose to his usurped office.

Huxley

It feels rather busy in here for a crew of people meant to be shutting down an operation. Please show me what steps you are taking to call back those planes.

General Mitchell

Sir, it's not like snapping your fingers. It is a complex equation...with many variables. The miscalculation of anyone of them could create a situation worse than we wanted.

Huxley

I didn't really want any of this from the beginning.
I understand this plan is very important to you,

And I understand that you think you are doing a very noble thing...And yes...I had previously come to agree with you. That, however, was a decision made in a fever of fear...

A great mistake too often made.

But I am no longer fearful.

And today is not the day, General.

General Mitchell
I don't think you understand the full breadth of the situation!

Huxley
I understand more than you'll ever know, General. I want this to stop...right here... right now.
That is all the understanding you need.

General Mitchell
It's not that simple

Huxley
It is indeed that simple.
I said stop. You Stop.
Where are we with getting those planes back?

General Mitchell
That is proving more complicated than I originally thought.

Huxley
More complicated than you thought...or more complicated because you haven't called them back...and you're just pretending to work...as is everyone in this room.

You don't become president by not knowing when you're having the wool pulled over your eyes. I know how the game is played...I got to where I am...because I know how the game is played...

General Mitchell
Well...
OK...no sir...I have not called them back...because I don't believe that is the right course of action.

Huxley
You don't believe it, or you know it to be right?

General Mitchell
I know it.

Huxley
And how can you know it?
How many times have you sat around the fire?

General Mitchell
The...hell...are you...?

Huxley
I have felt what happens...I have been to the woods and on the open road. Made to face and touch the bodies...bound and pulled...and thrown back into the sea, returning from its depths, defeating the cold and the dark.

General Mitchell
Uh, huh?...
And you have consulted with your advisers as well, I assume?

Huxley
You could say that.

They helped me find my way.
They always do.

General Mitchell
Right…forgive me sir, but I took years to create this
operation…just in case some technologically induced
situation…such, that we find ourselves in at present, actually
occurred.

It happened, and now we are here…upon the precipice.

It is my time.
It is why I exist
And it is everything the world needs right now.
You need me.
We need, Dewdrop.

Huxley
General…

General Mitchell
So, forgive me if I am a bit less than excited, to find our
elected commander continually gone at key moments.
You were very certain about giving this the green
light…then…he's nowhere to be found…until, suddenly…he
appears...with three ancient, and notably dead people.
My God…this is more disastrous than the Canada offensive!
You and your dream consults…

Well I've had enough. And you said that you have just
returned from inside the sea…what's that all about…?

Huxley
Oh, it's…

General Mitchell
I don't actually care...but, please tell any of us here in this room...why we should be heeding your orders. You've obviously lost it.

Lieutenant II
You're a danger to the future of our world!

General Mitchell
Shut up.
You're a danger to the future of our world, Hux!

Huxley
We can save it all, General. Nothing has to be erased.

General Mitchell
This is our fate either way.
Remember...
If we don't do this...

All Personnel in Room
Somebody else will!

Chorus
Rising tall, upon two enigmatic feet
Acquiring eternity, no more against time to compete
Arising from the grasses, a separation from all previously known
Impetuously onward, metamorphosing, into to a fragile keystone

General Mitchell
This was our fate from the beginning
A losing game we are committing

Our prosperity continually usurped for survival
This path of an end, is the way to great revival

Chorus
And this did lead to monsters of invention, and annihilation
Our best selves forever in abdication
With them gone, nothing to fill the void
A wandering nobody, can sculpt the sea; totality erased and
destroyed

General Mitchell
And if our steps remain true
We will not end, but usefully start anew
This doctrine and operation must be tested
Forgetting how to live, it will bring back life, resurrected

Chorus
In a constant battle, sometimes victorious, sometimes the
vanquished
To arise again, shaking the guilt and anguish
Picking up where we left off, inhaling a 'never again', we do
devote
Our steps forever upon the asymptote

Huxley
Since time immemorial it has happened
An unfortunate end was a new paradise imagined
Our great beginning built upon chronicles buried and decaying
I will not allow this ground more bones left laying

Chorus
Beginnings and endings, trading places in perpetuity
Recorded in the stone book for eternity
Nothing can stay, permanence a folly of mind

But only one path of many, if walked today, leaves nothing
behind

Huxley
In our hands we hold the chisel, into stone recorded
Will our story be triumphant, or a tale to be abhorréd
Our decisions this day will tell the next ones who we really were
No more will I return to the the fire; the raft, the breath, the sea,
today will not recur

Chorus
We will never truly know
The exact persons long ago
Belonging to the hands imprinted
On the walls of the cave, wherein our world they invented
The connection remains, that we cannot outgrow
Another us was there aeons ago
Their story today, continues to remain
The dead will live, the fire and the endless winter, in its final
refrain

Huxley
We know for certain, that we're the faces
The sculpting, draughting hands, leaving august traces
Recording without ending
No more pasts contending
The monsters of imagination
Today will be subdued to mythicization
The plinths will not fall into an indifferent ground
Onward! Onward! No longer our voluntary blindness will hang
our heads down!

General Mitchell
We are all on the same side here, sir

Huxley
I sincerely hope so.
I'll say this one final time...shut this down.

General White
Too many variables!

Colonel Lewis
Not enough time.

General White
It has already begun.

Huxley
There's always the opportunity to undo a wrong.
You just need to want to.

Lieutenant I
Planes are 30 minutes from their targets, sir.

General Harris
Just call it off! This is ludicrous.
I will not continue to be a part of this.

General Mitchell
Oh, really...where are you going to go? You know how this operation plays out...you know the phases. You want to be out there when it happens...be my guest...I'm out of contact with them, and they'll be dropping their payloads soon.
There is no time.
A new world is starting.
This is not my doing.
It was put in motion the day we sharpened our first stone.

We knew this day would come...what side of it would you rather be on?

Lieutenant I
Ten minutes...

Narrator
A feeble transmission. A radio yearning to make contact. A distressing and garbled static message.

Pilot I
Generals, Generals!
Who's there?
Anyone?

Huxley
Captain, this is the President.
Captain?
Where are you? What is your name, son?

Pilot I
Can no one hear us?
...they can't hear us...

Pilot II
Just keep talking.
Someone, somewhere, is always listening.

Pilot I
We were met with massive resistance.
I thought, no one was to know we were coming...
What have you sent us into!

Narrator
Explosions muffled through an ill-working radio.

Pilot II
Lost the engine
Lost the...

General Mitchell
How could they know we're coming?

Major Mills and Dr. Palmer
There are more eyes watching you...than you'll ever know.

Dr. Palmer
The man in the machine knew the plan from the beginning.
It blinded you.

Major Mills
It saw right into you.
The man in the machine was waiting...for you, General.

Pilot II
We're going down!

General Mitchell
That's nonsense! How could a...see into, or...know...and make a plan...multiple and varied contingent plans?

Huxley
End this General.

General Mitchell
Gladly...Lieutenant, send in the other planes.
Send in the real cookers.

Huxley
I meant call off the operation!

General Mitchell
You said end this. I'm ending it...once and for all.

Huxley
Shut it down.
Bring them back...now!

General Mitchell
The operation can't be shut down now sir.
The planes have arrived at their targets...you heard it yourself.
Bombs are falling as we speak.

You've begun a noble war...you're doing the right thing...

Huxley
General Wesley Mitchell, I am relieving you of your command, effective immediately. Your blind ambitions have tripped upon the feet of fear.

This path will only make you a momentary master...it will fade away...it cannot stay. Who will you be, if you continue this path? Who will you be... after the blood is mopped up?

You know the answer...and yet you do not relent from this path.

General Mitchell
No...enough!
That's enough!
This is all such nonsense!
This operation will continue with or without you.
I will not be undone!
We are doing the right thing...the world will be free from the prison of these weapons...this is the only way to untie the knot.

Thucydides
There are other paths.

General Mitchell
No!
Our feet have already set out.
We will walk the entire path until the end.
We will not be undone.

Democritus
Some paths go on forever, without an end.
Imagine a road that seems endless,
Then imagine that it is.

Huxley
It's over. You are relieved of your duties.

General Mitchell
But the breeding program!
We must reach the final phase…it's imperative!

We stay the course. It's the only way.

General White
We stay the course. It's the only way.

Colonel Lewis
We stay the course. It's the only way.

Chorus
Stay the course, ol' man…
Imperative to the program!

We will not deviate from what we began…
The new world depends upon the program!

The new world, by damn...
Founded by the program!

Narrator
A strong and confident motion of a singular hand, the permissive sign for someone awaiting your command, to enter, or come closer, to receive secretive information. The sound of hammering boots approach, and Huxley being of his age, office, and experience, knows very well that the particular pitch he hears, is of military boots. Authoritative, implimentative, and foreboding. Whilst the Greeks remain unaware of any impending situation, Huxley is all too aware. In him, the same feelings when surrounded by the living dead, noosing him and hurling him into the dark sea; the horrific tachycardia, the withdrawal of nerves from the skin, the coldness that washes over, retracting his eyes and mind. He knows he will be led away, usurped, and replaced. Is there a chance to fight? No. There is not. Not here. Not now. When the staccatoed boots come to a stop behind him, he turns to see in perfect clarity, the same face with exposed skull, as from out on his road.

Huxley
Ahh!

Narrator
Quickly reclaiming himself, he touches the face of a very much alive, member of the military police, young and naïve, a boy, mindlessly doing a job. There is another motion of the hand from General Mitchell, declaratively implicating to other officers in the room to come over and lend intimidation to the act of presidential arrest.

General Mitchell
I am afraid today, it will be the other way around, sir. We, the undersigned...hereby...officially inform you, President Garrick Huxley, that we are henceforth relieving you of your duties as president, as well as Commander of the Armed Forces. You will find the signatures of all in this room.

Huxley
Can you actually do that?

General Harris
That can't be valid?

General Mitchell
It is signed.
It is written...so it is!
And it is embossed as well.

You are no longer mentally fit to control the office of your election. Our current situation has proven too much for you.
Your constant absences, in this situation as well as the previously disastrous Canada Offensive, were of particular concern...where is it that you go?

Never mind! I no longer care.
We are upon the precipice of our greatest canyon...
And you dress up actors, parading them as advisors of the ancient past...thinking it would fool us...teach us some sort of lesson...ha!

Huxley
Please General. They are very much real.

General Mitchell
They are actors, please...

Thucydides, Democritus, Zeno
We are who we said.
We are what we wrote.
Unfortunate, it was not read.

General Mitchell
Yes, I am sure it was a real page-turner...

Belmont
We are here, because they were.
Don't kill the dead!

Dr. Palmer
They allowed us to vanquish death!
Because those before them allowed the same.
Don't take that away.

Major Mills
Killing the present, will kill the dead...erased forever
Ask yourself who you are...what is it you actually want?

General Mitchell
Thank you, Major.
Looks like this will be a larger haul than previously expected.

Narrator
Taking out the official document, General Mitchell hastily
grabs a pen and scrawls more names onto the page, reciting
them in mumbled vociferousness.

General Mitchell
General Harris...
Ambassador...pshh...James...Belmont
Doctor...Ruth Palmer
Major T.W... Mills...

We require a few more cuffs if you please. ...these four, and those three whoevers...

Oh, Hux...no, no...you get to stay. Let's both witness the creation of a new world. I assure you; you will have your place in it. I want you to see.

I've saved you a seat.

Narrator
Thucydides, Democritus, and Zeno, having lived aeons beyond themselves, successfully utilizing the simple and intrinsic tools which give our species the ability to do away with death, are for the first time in the totality of their lives, afraid that they will die the final death.

Thucydides, Democritus, Zeno
No! No! No!

General Mitchell
It is time for the past...to die.

IV.V

Narrator

The Greeks, thrown while still cuffed, into the war room with all other allies of President Huxley, are hurled to their knees and finally de-cuffed, out of some remaining humanity; though fleeting as quickly as smoke from a match, as they are then rather inhumanely, kicked down upon the cuffs' removal. The doors slam behind them. Hinge-shrieking echoes of perhaps a final-end. Before any of them can rise to their feet, their eyes look up. The totality of their collective vision is consumed by the images of the stone book. There is nothing else visible.

As physical pain begins to spread throughout their bodies, with the anguish of being on the losing side of a battle, perhaps the last battle, there is no conversation in the room; not of sympathy, not of consolation. Keeping their emptiness internal, because they know full well that it is inside of everyone in the war room; an unspoken knowing that while very much alive at present, momentarily, could come not only an ending of themselves, but an annihilation of the totality of existence. There is no need to put it into the imperfectness of words.

On a side buffet bench in the room, still perfectly arranged, pristinely clean, white ceramic cups and saucers, and a copper carafe of fresh coffee. A simple and essential domestic pleasure, contradictory to the abstractness and insanity of what is being discussed and implemented just one room over. Without words, and in total silence; a benefit of the confidentiality of the war room, cups are filled, and seats taken. They drink coffee in silence, as if they were doing so, early in a morning, when children are still asleep, and a first snow is falling.

The prisoners mill about the war room, having enjoyed a peaceful, seated cup of coffee, they refill their cups, and approach the stone book. A luxury they have not had before; to look at great art up-close, all while enjoying their coffee. Something in a museum, no one, not even the most expert and intimate caretakers of the work, would be allowed; but when existence is upon a horizon of erasure, rules can be discarded. Belmont looks at a scene on the relief, as if hoping that it will give him some last-ditch prophecy. The stone book, in its way, does give something very useful to him. Not a pictorial answer to some grand questions, but rather, an opportunity. The stone book is a powerful presence sculpted in a powerful material; but all things have weaknesses, and stone, despite our preconceptions of it, can also be as fragile and transient as glass. Belmont notices the beginnings of a long crack in the stone. Running his fingers along it, blowing away dust that has filled its shallow valley, making it visible with great definition. He knows that this simple crack in a piece of stone, could save not only himself and those in the room, but if done with calculation, stealth, and strength, could save the entire world, and all of history, thanks to the convenient idiot, who knowingly or not, placed the crack; more than likely a nobody, who may change back the currents of the sea, before they are even shifted, and will never know that his buffoonery, could save the world, and yet, probably will never be recorded as a most poignant impetus of any hope of a future.

The long silence of anguish and dejection is broken by Ambassador Belmont, with the timbre of a million mosquitos crammed into a single atom.

Belmont
If they will not listen to history...
We will crush them with it.

Narrator
Belmont pushes, kicks, and rocks back-and-forth the piece of stone from the corner of the relief. It relinquishes itself crashing to floor and smashing into an array of different sized pieces. One such shattered piece, he picks up admiring its sharpened edge. Holding it, Belmont is amazed at how well it fits into the natural shape of his dominant, striking hand. He grips it tighter, and rehearsing in deliberate movements, in sluggish time, the practiced moves of effective attack. An intrinsic actionable knowledge still inside us, from our moribund survivalism. The room in shocked silence, observe Belmont, and in likewise thought, including heroes who willingly traveled from an ancient era, know the only way to resolve the situation. The great path of intrepidness that began four million years ago, anxiously, accidentally, and eruditely evolving into our age; an age of light-speed communication, the ability to stare with clarity to other worlds, and the creation of weaponry utilizing the smallest essence of our universe, our delicate existence, that through our most ancient and insurmountable survival attribute, foolishly shifted our collective feet to a precipice of unimaginable doom, a doom that may now be overcome, with sharpened stones. The singular implement that set us apart from our last common ancestors, the very object that sent us from the savannahs to the cosmos.

Filled with the swelling joy and norepinephrine of survival and reconnection to our most ancient rudimentary selves, the entire room uses what impromptu tools are available, to dismantle the great stone book. Breaking along its veins, it begins to come down to the floor in dangerously lethal implements, leaving larger pieces left as is, to use for the breaking of doors, or if it came to it, to put out of misery, a wounded, and immobile victim of their attack, perhaps even, if it came to it, one of their own.

A cache of weaponry now at their disposal, they are ready to dispose of it. As well as anyone that is on the wrong side of history. And that is everyone who refused to listen to history, when it was present in the room with them. The guards at the door of Huxley's former office do not know what is momentarily coming their way, nor in the greater scheme, do they really care. Though trained to follow orders and disregard independent thought, even in the most nervous and anxious of times, no amount of training to extinguish our natural protective instincts could uphold the realities of total annihilation on mankind's horizon. They simply stand at the door, and hope for the best. That is all anyone in the world is doing right now. Standing at some real or proverbial door, looking out of windows, and inhaling large final breaths of good air, while a few chosen people, make decisions, and we hope that they are not maniacs. But the guards' inner thoughts and hopes for the future are not known to those infused with the chemicals of survival. In total silence, the imprisoned motion to each other, the sign to begin their operation. Packed with makeshift bandoliers and pockets full of sharpened stones, moving through an interim door in the war room they peer around the corner to what was, until recently, the President's office. Removing their shoes and all unnecessary clothing, they gather their collective breath, perhaps the last unpolluted breath of their lives, and perhaps one of the last deep inspirations in our collective histories. Making the signal, and with the stealth of stalking cats, come up behind the guards who are a few feet off the doors, and in perfect unison make elegantly forceful draws across the neck of each guard, like a razor through dough, fully risen before going into the oven, the surface tension broken, and internal becoming external. Allowing the weight of the guards to slink into themselves and break their falls, keeping secret their deed, as well as their close proximity to the nerve center.

Large rocks are now hurled at the door to Huxley's old office. The battle is underway. The sound of manic hammering boots, running in all directions; assuming their places to defend, a sound that is unmistakable, the sound of a prepared retaliation. And, if there is one thing known to those beginning a war, it is that the most rudimentary weapons can stand strongly against the most technologically advanced. For in militaristic technology comes hubris and laziness, but with sticks and stones, comes an unshakable and religious purpose; a thing that cannot be broken, a will that cannot be toppled. Inside the office, muffled panic of desperate commands to proceed to the final act; regardless of the proper phases and steps in between.

General Mitchell
Hurry…this is it. Time for the big ones!
Begin the launch sequence!

General White
Now!

Narrator
A rock breaks part of the door. The tiniest beacon of light and hope appears through, and just like the stone book exposing its weakness and vulnerability, so has the door to the makeshift command center. If only they had chosen to be able to look at the stone book, to be in the secure room, this would not have occurred; in their confidence, they thought it would be easy, that history once shackled, humiliated, and dragged away,

would not be able to return. Then another rock, and another, exposing more light, more weakness, and more vulnerability.

General Mitchell
Has the code been entered?

Colonel Lewis
Almost, sir.

General Mitchell
Hurry up damnit!
Do it!

Narrator
Another rock at exactly the right place, exposing enough light, enough space, for a brave someone to get through and penetrate the command center.

Colonel Lewis
Code entered, sir.

General Mitchell
Begin the launch sequence!

General White
We need the president's confirmation code.

General Mitchell
Give me the code, Hux

Huxley
Never.

Narrator
At the same time as Huxley's refusal, General Harris, grasping two perfectly sharpened stones, one from his storage, and one stone which was tested and proven upon an unsuspecting guard, the blood, beginning to dry. His grip cracks the fragile coffee-red shell staining the rock, and blood flows on the General's hand. He crouches down towards the hole broken into the door. He enters. Waiting are soldiers, believing in nothing but a cause they were instructed to believe in. Three gunshots ring out. A silence. Then, an oppressively heavy thud, a singular sound, no reverberations, no auxiliary or follow-up sounds, just one solid body thumped on the ground. The remaining bury the pain of a departed, and continue. Another rock. And another.

General Mitchell
Hux! Give it to me.

General White
He must keep it on him at all times.
He must have it.

Huxley
You'll have to kill me.

Lieutenant I
Here it is. Sewn into the lining of his jacket.

General Mitchell
Enter this code now!

Lieutenant II
Sir.

Narrator
Another slyly enters through the cracked door, this time more stealthily; due to which and much like with the initial guards, an element of surprise works against a soldier, and internal becomes external, and no scream is heard, but rather a gargle; a choking. Before the body is to the ground, the gun from his waistband is taken, pointed, and used; three times in three directions. A single person took four. But with that came the price of alerting his presence in an already tiny room. He didn't see where it came from, just the sound, the lightning-quick crack, then a peaceful silence, in a world, still, for the moment, intact.

Lieutenant II
Code entered.

General Mitchell
Launch! Launch!

General White
Beginning the launch sequence…

Colonel Lewis
Launch sequence. Confirmed.

General Mitchell
The keys! The keys!
You've got to turn the keys!

Every remaining person storms the room. The final push. Clumsy bullets spray the room, and stones striking with calculated maneuver. The repeated singular thuds of the chapters of lives ending. Codes entered; two keys inserted but remaining unturned. The echoes of bullets and stones fading, are replaced by the delicate sounds of fast, deep, rapidly anxious breaths, from only two remaining and equally anxious men. A usurped President, holding a sharpened stone, picked from the graveyard that was at one time his office, dripping with the blood of people that were his friends and subordinates only moments ago. A delusional General, desperately clinging to a pistol, with the malaligned intentions of a zealot. A quick glance down, and an expedient check of its insides tells him he has one bullet remaining, and two keys between them. A thumb clicks a hammer into place, a hand tightens on a rock, oozing blood between fingers. The entirety of history and collective futures lay in between two men with the exasperated panting breaths of lions. Two hearts beating with timpanic oppressiveness. Four lungs inhaling smoke and blood.

Thank You

This book is only possible due to the support of many. To my wife Emily, and son Ansel; you are everything to me, I am infinitely thankful for you both, your love and support keeps me going every day. A special thank you to my parents Mark and Jane Morrow, I owe you both everything; your love and support over the course of my life has allowed me to walk many amazing paths. Thank you to Lee Alan Morrow for your generous readings of drafts, your critique, and unending support during the writing process. Thank you, Jim and Shirley Wagner, for your support through the many years. Thank you to my sister, Megan. Thank you to Gladys 'Grandma Fargo' Morrow, Kathleen Marriott Johnson, and 'Papa' Bill Johnson, though you are now gone, the people you were, shaped me into who I am, and who I continue to strive to be. Thank you to all family present and long past; your stories inspire me to create; to add to our compendium of stories without end.

Many languages are included in this work, and it took the efforts of these generous people to have them represented. A sincere thank you to: Angelica Fritzvold for the Norwegian translation; Tolu Akinwole for the Yoruba translation; Brett Graham for the Māori translation; Susana Maria Antunes for the Portuguese translation; Yuko Kojima Wert for the Japanese translation; Viktorija Bilic for the German translation; Maud Roset for the French translation; Macarena Franco for the Spanish translation, Isabella Livorno for the Italian translation, Michael Zimmerman for the Potawatomi translation, Pearly Nguyen for the Vietnamese translation; Xingwei (Sylvie) Cui for the Mandarin translation.